I0748377

INTELLECT + LUNACY = IVY LEAGUE

Studying Hard & Partying Harder
at the World's Foremost University

Jason W. Park, PhD

First Edition

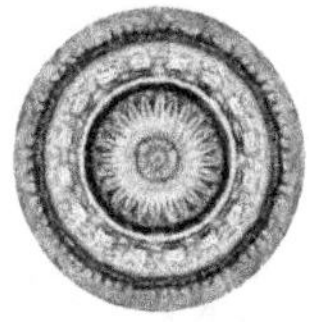

Manhattan Beach, California

INTELLECT + LUNACY = IVY LEAGUE
Studying Hard & Partying Harder
at the World's Foremost University
by Jason W. Park, PhD

Collected Wisdom Publishing
2711 N. Sepulveda Blvd. #282
Manhattan Beach, CA 90266

Author's Note: This is a work of fiction. Names, characters, businesses, places, events and incidents are either the products of the author's imagination or used in a fictitious manner. Any resemblance to actual persons, living or dead, or actual events is purely coincidental.

Cover design by Deloris (www.fiverr.com/prodesignsx)
Editing by Robin Quinn (www.writingandediting.biz)
Author photograph by JMin
Book Layout © 2014 BookDesignTemplates.com

Library of Congress Cataloging-in-Publication Data

Intellect + Lunacy = Ivy League : Studying Hard & Partying Harder at the World's Foremost University / Jason W. Park, PhD – 1st ed.

ISBN-13: 978-0-692-72222-0
LCCN/PCN: 2016908679

Dedicated to

My Loving Parents

CONTENTS

PROLOGUE

OCTOBER 15, 1994

Green lasers shot through the undercover darkness of a machine-made fog blanketing the warehouse space, the spot rented for the night's rave in an industrial neighborhood in Boston. The house/techno music thudded in my overwhelmed ears at a constant 140 Beats Per Minute, on and on, repeatedly, never-ending, unstoppable, over and over again. On the dancefloor, I picked up shadowy glimpses of bodies gyrating to the beat, but I was in no mood for dancing. It was all I could do to just walk around and take drags off a lit cigarette to contain my anxiety.

As I paced, I inspected my wristwatch, the time barely visible in the light. In the last half-hour no spiritual awakening had overcome me. I had washed down a quarter of the XTC pill 30 minutes ago with a swig of water, then another one-fourth 15 minutes after that with more *agua*, and yet I wandered around the tame outskirts of the party, feeling like the only uninitiated virgin in the entire red-light district of Amsterdam. I flicked my still-lit butt off into outer space, followed its glow to the floor, and ground it out under my foot before lighting up another. I was running out of drugs, out of time, out of water, out of cigarettes and out of patience…

And yet there was indeed something there, an underlying current of elevated mood, stirring from the depths, as if something were ready to punch through the surface of my ennui. I kept walking around the warehouse space, so as not to seem like a loser. I had just taken another drag on my cigarette when, from out of nowhere, my drug dealer Sam bumped into me.

"Sam, I took half and I don't feel anything yet!" I yelled above the noise.

He yelled back at me: "Just take the rest of it!"

In desperate resignation I pulled the remaining half-pill from my wallet and chomped with vengeance on it. I retched at the sheer bitterness of its purity, very glad for the bottled water to wash all of the disintegrating particles down my throat. I tossed the empty bottle off into a corner of the stage, towards the stacks of speakers emitting painfully loud melodies of fighter-jet sonic booms and the rattling of machine-gun beats.

Now that I had sealed my fate, I parked myself off-center on the dancefloor, surrounded by sweaty hot strangers, all alone in the middle of a crowd. I had lost touch with my crew, I had lost touch with my dealer, I was lost, lost, completely and utterly lost...

And then, suddenly I sensed a sharp crack towards the back of my head, as if white-hot fire were sweeping from my medulla through the cerebellum and up to the cerebrum, forcing me to suck in air. I squinted inwardly as my brain began to cave in, like a galactic supernova collapsing under its own weight, until my gray matter imploded completely and reverse-exploded outward, radiating white-hot Jesus rays. I doubled forward to brace myself, hands on knees for support, and held my breath. *Wait, I can't see!*

In my hollow chest, my heart thudded mesmerizingly and at one with the dance rhythm, the same BOOM! BOOOM!! BOOOOM!!! BOOOOOM!!!! which had been so unenthralling just seconds ago. A wellspring of joy inched up to my neck and over my chin until it contorted my lower face in a Cheshire Cat's grin. An unbearably intense 30 seconds later, the surge became a less extreme but more constant stream of white-hot radiance. My vision returned, and I exhaled as my hands-on-knees became a hands-in-air while I yowled wildly and joined the rest of the revelers on the dancefloor.

The high cured me of my afflictions: visions of Seventh Heaven shot through me as irritability melted into serenity, and sadness transitioned into bliss. I skipped around the dance floor like a youngster on a playground, and regrouped with my Dealer-For-Life in front of the DJ booth, bear-hugging and high-fiving him. Sam guffawed silently in the ultra-loudness, the lasers making his face glow green in that darkly lit warehouse, then wagged his finger and yelled into my ear, “See, Jay? I told you so!”

CHAPTER ONE

T-MINUS HIGH SCHOOL AND COUNTING…

"Are you nervous?"

Those three words raced across the private phone line from Cambridge to Pittsburgh, like a submarine's bright ping slicing through the murky depths of the ocean, then echoed back and forth within my mind. Like in a near-death experience, where everything was at stake, my entire life flashed before my eyes as I tightly clutched the phone in one sweaty hand and steadied myself against the kitchen counter with the trembling other. My mother hovered right next to me, wanting to hear every word uttered. My brother Justin paced back and forth on the squeaky wooden floor, barely able to contain his anxiety. My father waited for word at his office, expecting a regular report at constant intervals. Even the cicadas momentarily silenced their droning while the wind died and the trees stopped their rustling, as if to get a better hearing of the upcoming verdict. I stared off into space and thought: *it ALL comes down to this…*

It was September 1992, and I was talking to an admissions representative from Harvard University about the status of my Early Action application. So what exactly was at stake here? Could it have been about whether all that drilling for the Advanced Placement exams in History, Chemistry, English and Math had finally paid off? Whether it had made sense for me to rudely wrest the title of Editor-in-Chief of the student paper from an unambitious classmate, all to simply pad my resume? Whether sweating it out at lacrosse was evidence enough to the committee that I was an athlete with promise? Whether enduring all those stormy piano lessons from a punitive taskmaster would impress some impresario at Harvard that I had enough talent for the classical music world? Whether all that tutoring and practicing to score a personal best 1530 on the (old) Scholastic Aptitude Test was enough of a complement for my all-A school grades? Actually, at stake were all these things, and then some. The issue, all in all, was whether I had gained entrance into the university that for the last 350 years had established itself as the most preeminent, most predominant, and most prestigious institute of higher education in the world. As I pressed the phone to my perspiring ear, I declared to myself, *Harvard, here I come!*

But that was only half of it. There was another side of myself that had me worried silly. Had I dumbed myself down too much toking up to Jimmy Cliff and Bunny Wailer, or traipsing off into the woods to get high on a makeshift inhaler pipe? Had I killed too many brain cells pounding beers to Rush and Crosby, Stills, Nash and Young, and cavorting on golf courses at midnight? What about the time idled beating a monster boss on Sega Genesis's Sonic the Hedgehog? To many of my high school classmates, and sometimes even to me, no future was no problem, academics were no-priority, and scoring was about securing an eighth-ounce of marijuana, not putting a lacrosse ball in a wide-open net. *Game over! Here comes the rejection of my life!*

So was I nervous? "A little bit..." I replied weakly.

The admissions representative giggled in response. *What?! Hey, that's like laughing at a funeral! This was no time for levity. Harvard obviously hired sadists to handle the phones...*

Brief pause..."Congratulations, Mr. Kim! You've been accepted to Harvard University's Class of 1997 under the Early Action program. Shortly you'll receive a packet in the mail formally extending the University's invitation and, moreover, requesting your response to the University's invitation, from the Dean of Admissions and Financial Aid, Dr. William Fitzsimmons."

The phone connection had delivered the voice of an omniscient, omnipotent goddess, beckoning me onward and past the pearly gates of Heaven. The trees outside in the forest surrounding our house roared their approval as the wind picked up again, and the cicadas voiced their kudos as they resumed their droning. After thanking the caller, I returned the moist headset back to its base, leaving a sweaty palm print on the back of it, steadied myself with both hands on the kitchen counter, then turned to Mom and grinned. "Mom, I got in…!"

An overjoyed smile appeared on her face and tears welled up in her eyes. "Oh, Jay!"

Justin stopped pacing and started doing a victory dance.

I then called my father: "Dad, I got into Harvard!" He never left the office at midday unless there was an emergency, such as one of us being sick or a death in the extended family. But this too counted as a special occasion. He turned the 40-minute one-way commute from the University of Pittsburgh's Oakland campus into a 20-minute zoom back to the house in the Fox Chapel suburbs. I met him outside on the driveway. We embraced. I had never seen my father so happy.

And as for me, how did I feel? I was in fact quite relieved. All that hard work had finally paid off, after a delayed gratification of 17 years. A relatively unknown public high-school student from an immigrant middle-class family hailing from a medium-size American big city had just distinguished himself in the most audacious manner. The entire universe, the whole cosmos, the world order, was with me now, revolving and circling around me, no longer my chasing after it. In this race, I had reached the finish line way out in first place, with time to spare.

Or so it seemed. In fact, high school was just one leg of a larger race, and college would require me to prove myself yet again. In high school, I had become acquainted with the cliques dividing the student body: high-achiever versus abject slacker; straightedge abstainer versus hardcore partier; isolated individual versus social butterfly. By high school's end, I had learned to internalize these conflicts, and by college's end, I would learn to resolve them. But unbeknownst to me as a high school senior, looking brightly ahead, the four years at Harvard would be some of the toughest of my life.

*****

A high-school Friday...

...and I was studying with the half-a-dozen straight-A soon-to-be valedictorians, of which I was one, a rather uncomfortably pushy cohort, each of us trying to outdo the other. We interacted in school because we had the same classes: Advanced Placement Math, English, Chemistry and so on, so we learned to hang out with each other. In fact, from Monday morning to Friday afternoon, I would enjoy associating with them, as I had my assigned duties to parents and to teachers. But as soon as the final bell rang at 2:30 PM on a Friday afternoon, I would disband from them until Monday.

On the bus ride home, I sat next to Jennifer, a super-hot, very attractive classmate.

"Hey, Jen, do you have my cigs?" I queried coyly.

"Yeah, right here!" she replied, whipping out a sealed pack of Camel Lights and handing it to me. We had an agreement: she would pick up cigarettes from the local gas station with my allowance. It was a silly arrangement. After all, why didn't I just go with her or by myself? Why would I make the girl go? But she didn't mind committing a crime for me, and I as usual had to get home, where mommy ruled the roost.

Still, the plan gave her an excuse to jump off the bus with me near the local Campbell's Lake to light up together and be with Nature. The mid-afternoon sun glittered off the ripples of the bobbing, floating surface of the brackish water, and touched with gold the grass, weeping willows and pines on the far side. She and I would talk obliquely about how she wasn't rich and I wasn't white, about how she had no family and I was frustrated with mine, and about how she oftentimes felt like a dumb blonde and I felt stereotyped as a Asian dork. We got along well, despite the fact that we had absolutely nothing in common, other than our shared humanity and mutual alienation from others. She was a good person and a good friend.

But then again, no rest for the wicked! I had to leave her and rush off for the grass and mud of the lacrosse field to showcase my athletic prowess in matches against opposing high schools. Lacrosse was the only contact sport that favored my flighty 5'9", 150-lbs. frame. For American football I just wasn't big or bulky enough. But with "lax," I could easily walk on in my sophomore year as a midfielder, even though my parents had never heard of the sport before ("Lacrosse? Is it religious?"). In a one-on-one against a beefy enemy midfielder, I tirelessly poke-, slap- and cross-checked him out of bounds, to my teammates' delighted heckling, sending him careening headfirst into a border of plastic orange safety posts half-submerged in a muddy puddle lining the playing field. He crumpled off-balance into all this mess, splashing watery mud all over himself and flinging the posts this way and that as if he'd been spat there, with the ball shooting up out of his stick pocket way up in the air, to the huge cheers of my teammates, and then to their raucous jeers when the referee's whistle issued a "Tweet!"

And so by 6 PM or so, lacrosse would end. But the festivities had just begun! Come that night, I would seek out kindred spirits such as Larry, a teammate of mine, who had a wonderful source for some great weed: his parents! Every now and then, he would sneak a few choice buds from their stash for a little get-together at his adult-vacated abode. Meanwhile, another accomplice secured a connection to a local beer distributor and ordered a half-barrel of Milwaukee's Best for the occasion. The girls would arrive shortly afterwards, the stereo would blast rock and reggae, and *voila,* we had a party!

Upon inhaling the harsh cough-inducing fumes from a metal pipe, I sensed a pressured emptiness in my head like an inflated balloon, as the THC moved through my brain. Cottonmouth left me thirsty for fluids, and combined with the munchies, I'd become motivated to storm Larry's kitchen for junk food and move on to the living room for a beer. Soon even everyday conversation became intense and profound. The music of Bob Marley and Peter Tosh sounded as if it were beamed down from outer space, or as if it were emanating from the inside center of your skull.

The beer flowed freely from the bumper on the half-barrel, and I imbibed generously. I liked beer. Why go down when you can go up, up, up? I didn't want to feel sad anymore. The alcohol, despite its depressant effect, gave me a super-sloshed, hee-haw happy high.

Someone changed the soundtrack and now the stereo blared Led Zeppelin and Pink Floyd. I swayed clumsily to the music, which sounded even better then than when sober. The bubbly froth of the golden-white liquid called me to raise my glass to my lips over, and over, and over, and over again. Some Friday nights I just enjoyed the buzz; other times I would end the night kneeling before the porcelain throne, sick to my stomach.

*****

The next Saturday morning...

"Jay, wake up," Mom would cajole us, and if that didn't work, "Come on, gather your strength!" she would yell into our bedrooms as she prowled the hallway.

If I heard her say that, then it was too late. Consciousness entered and registered in my brain: *Oh, God. It can't be, but it is...* Saturday morning, 7:30 AM, with a late fall, early winter chill seeping through my bedroom window, and still hungover from the night before. I just wanted to hide under the covers in bed. But, in my house, weekends were no less serious than school days, and perhaps they were even more intense, because school imposed a general structure of waking up, doing things and taking breaks, whereas on the weekends the motivation had to come from the inside.

"Jay, Justin! *Jungshin jum che-dee-oh*!" Mom shouted, reverting to Korean in excitement.

On any given school-year Saturday, Dad would lead the charge, shuttling to and from his office at the University of Pittsburgh's business school, taking no break from his weekday schedule. Meanwhile Mom taxied me to and from piano lessons at the neighboring (and more prestigious, of course) Carnegie Mellon University. Justin played in the Pittsburgh Symphony Youth Orchestra, and Mom also took him along to practice sessions with his unwieldy cello in tow, a pricey little toy that made Dad very irritable when he saw it not being fully utilized.

But this particular Saturday was the date of the semester-ending piano recital, an unspeakable act of torture that I was compelled to participate in. I would get myself up there, onto the stage, in front of my adolescent peers, for their Asian parents of the city of Pittsburgh to point at, gossip about and publicly judge. My teacher, Mrs. Li, was Chinese and hogged up more than her fair share of resources and time from Carnegie Mellon's music program. Nearly all her students were East or Central Asian, whether Indian, Chinese, Korean or Japanese, with the occasional oddball Argentinian from South America. This was her preference because Mrs. Li knew that Asian parents pushed their kids and appreciated classical music. I vied for recital time with these other students, as I moved up the ranks in seniority, initially placed in the middle of the first recital program I first played in this sequence at age 11, then backwards towards the end of the recital program as I progressed towards age 18. It was constant tit-for-tat zero-sum competition for bragging rights for the parents, including Mom. I admit, I liked playing the piano and making music, but I also practiced for these recitals out of fear because I didn't want to make a fool of myself on stage, in public, for others to see. The fear of failure is a most unpleasant negative motivator, as I knew so well.

"Alright! I'll be there!" I dragged myself to the shower, feeling the hot water drip over my skinny adolescent body, wanting to stay in the warmth for a half-hour and not just five minutes, and out of the cold and freezing winter of Western Pennsylvania. Fearing parental rebuke, I jumped out and shivered through a pat-down with my towel, hurriedly getting into underwear and T-shirt, climbing into my ill-fitting suit, which I kept growing out of in high school. Too short in the legs, too tight in the crotch, feeling like a characterless corporate suit, my outfit was comprised of a drab navy blazer with a nondescript tie hanging down the front of an unflattering white button-down shirt, and down below, boring beige slacks and painfully uncomfortable penny loafers to complete the look. Getting in this garb was like pulling teeth!

Heading for the kitchen, I poured myself a bowl of cereal with milk and hurriedly chomped it down. This morning Mom didn't prepare breakfast for her family, as she was too busy preparing herself for the day ahead. Knowing that breakfast was merely delaying the inevitable, I finished my corn flakes and forced myself across the living room hall to the Steinway. Once seated, I jumpstarted with some scales and oh-so-boring "Hanon" piano exercises to get the blood running in the fingers. Then onto the piece itself: the first movement of Beethoven's Sonata in G major, Opus 14, Number 2, a piece that I actually liked, but that I had veritably practiced to death, until I could play it from rote memory, perhaps even a bit mechanically, in fact. Just like Asian educational methods with academics, it was the same with music: rote memorization, rule-based learning, and repetitive drilling!

"Jay! Time to go. Otherwise we'll be late!" Mom announced the final departure for the CMU campus. I shut the lid of the Steinway and headed out to the waiting car, emitting visible exhaust in the late fall/early winter, with Mom in the driver's seat…

*****

That Saturday afternoon…

…at Carnegie Mellon University's Fine Arts Building, a nervously endured 30-minute car ride away from home, we arrived to find the recital at the Alumni Concert Hall already underway, with the younger kids taking their turns on shorter, less complicated pieces. I was placed 20th out of a total program of 25, and the unlucky 13th was on stage. The wait was never easy, but for the time being I joined Mom in the audience and tried to enjoy the feeling of not being up there. I spied Mrs. Li in the very front row, engaged in barely subdued gesticulation, synchronized to the piece being played. The anxiety of anticipation caught up to me when the 17th student began playing. Mom shoved me away, and I skedaddled backstage and behind the last student in line. *Oh, boy, oh boy, how much of this do I have to bear?* Then the applause broke out and the 18th student went on. I heard the piano playing some unfamiliar tune that Mrs. Li had never taught me to play. I calmed myself: *in fifteen minutes, it'll all be over…until the next semester!* I laughed bitterly at my own joke, before applause broke out again, and the 19th student went on. The audience settled back down and the piano began to plunk out a now-familiar tune, Bach's Prelude and Fugue in C Minor from The Well-Tempered Clavier. *Oh yeah, I remember playing that one*…I ran the tune through my fingers, still having the muscle memory for it. And then…it was over, and the piano went silent, and the audience voiced its approval loudly.

Next came my turn. Now everything seemed to happen in slow-motion. I saw brief glimpses of the 19th student walking back to the stage side entrance, her face flushed and beaming…I walked carefully onto the black painted wooden stage, pock-marked with divots from heavy instrument feet…the sun came down in a soft haze from the glass ceiling, as if someone were watching over me…I positioned myself slightly in front of the piano, and bowed…the audience clapped loudly and then quieted in anticipation…I sat down on the bench and gripped it on opposite sides where the knobs turned to adjust the height while I tested its overall balance…I remembered the tune, again, Beethoven's Sonata in G Major, Op. 14, No. 2, and I saw it clearly in my mind's eye…I rested my hands on the keys in a now-familiar starting position: left hand in a lower G major triad, right hand thumb on middle D, right pinky an octave higher, middle finger on A-sharp, fourth finger on B, and index finger on F-sharp…I took a breath, and…AWAY WE GO…remembering the dynamics, the tempo, the pedaling, the technique, the balance between right and left hands, remembering everything I had learned and practiced up to that point… participating and observing at the same time, first-person and third-person simultaneously…not too much, not too little, but just right…navigating the repeated motifs, letting my hands fly…noting the key changes…and then resting on the last note…IT WAS OVER!

I got up from the bench with a huge smile of relief on my face. The audience erupted in applause and adulation, with a few outstanding hoots, whistles and cheers. Giddy with success, I could only see a swirl of faces in the brief moment before I bowed deeply and began walking off stage. *Where is Mom? Where is Mrs. Li? Where am I?* It was OK, I would regroup with them with me as a member of the audience, now fully relaxed and ready to enjoy Pianists 21 through 25.

*****

That Saturday evening…

…WHOOH!!! I'm FREEEEEE!!!

After the recital, Mom, seeing that I had done my time and paid my dues for now, decided to give me some much-needed R & R. In the waning sunlight of the late fall afternoon, she drove me away from Oakland's CMU campus and dropped me off in Lawrenceville, much to her chagrin. It was the "disreputable" part of Pittsburgh, a neighborhood completely beneath and off-limits to anybody from hoity-toity highfalutin Fox Chapel. But to me, it had a mysteriously strong pull as a vibrant, dynamic and energetic part of Pittsburgh.

I knocked on the door of one of the familiar row houses on Carnegie Street. The door slammed open and out popped a ruffian with a shock of blonde Calabrese hair and pale white German skin.

"WHAT'S UP, YOU PHATHEAD?!" he screamed elatedly as he reached to clasp my hand, a dazed, weed-induced grin appearing on his face.

"Hey, Donnie, ha ha," was my giddy, laugh-filled reply, vigorously returning the handshake and adding a hug on top.

Donnie was a free spirit. I appreciated his boisterous, no-holds-barred approach to life, his solid American rugged individualism, and his good-natured liberal-democratic tolerance. Being around him was a refreshing contrast to the tense silence and inhibiting strictness that at times characterized my adolescent home life.

I strolled into his house with my secret weapon at my side: an Acme freestyle skateboard with a pair of Gullwing trucks and four 50mm Spitfire wheels. Donnie went to get his own firearm, one of those old-school blimp-shaped boards with a pair of Independent trucks and four heavy, thick 95MM wheels. It was easier doing tricks—kickflips, heelflips, 180-shovits, ollies—with my Acme, but the board's footprint was small and it was harder simply to carve down the street. On Donnie's board, you could cruise down the sidewalk as if you were riding atop a huge stable platform, but because of its added weight, shape and size, you were limited in your repertoire of tricks. So it was a tradeoff.

"Let's roll, brother!" Donnie shouted out as he donned a flannel plaid collared shirt. I was still in my chinos and dress shirt, but I had changed into skate shoes.

"All right, man, let's hit the spot!"

We headed down the street to the bus stop, whereupon Donnie lit up a filtered cigarette. I bummed one off him since I hadn't been able sneak my own pack past Mom from home into my recital outfit. He registered faint annoyance when I grabbed for his lighter, too: *why am I paying for the rich kid's habit?* Anyhow, we both smoked like chimneys before the bus showed up, trying to impress any and all young teenage girls walking past. The big behemoth of a bus lumbered towards us as we flipped our cigarette butts out on the street and lined up to pile in. Of course, I didn't have exact change, and Donnie had to round up the fifty cents for me. As we headed back to the back of the bus, I could've sworn he was shaking his head in disbelief: *the kid lives in a quarter-million dollar house and he doesn't even have a single on him?* I was feeling sheepish and out-of-place in the dreary fluorescent buzz of public transportation. Nervous, I quietly carried on with Donnie while he half-listened, clearly more intent on the good-looking girl on the other side of the aisle.

We alighted right at the spot: Baum Boulevard and Melwood Avenue, near the Graffiti café a little ways up the street and a Kentucky Fried Chicken down in the opposite direction. From the northeast corner the concrete dipped down and back up on its way to some loading docks, forming a valley nearly 15 feet at its lowest depth, as if a sinkhole had hit but hadn't ruptured the street surface. It was undoubtedly of questionable structural integrity, but nevertheless a favorite target of local sidewalk surfers.

We boarded our respective aircraft and started flying. Donnie immediately got the idea, carving down into and up out of the valley, delicately touching the shuttered metal corrugated loading docks momentarily before reentering the lists to do battle with asphalt demons. He sailed back and forth on that static concrete ocean trough like a man possessed, as if he were chasing after a pot of gold at the end of a tarmac rainbow. As the darkness settled and the street lights went on, all I could see of him was his flannel plaid shirt fluttering in the breeze, his baggy jeans billowing outward, and his shock of blonde hair floating above the blacktop.

I, on the other hand, chose to work on my heelflip at the edge of the precipice, as I was too timid to fall in. I stood goofy-footed on my board, as I punched down with my left foot, popping the board up, and then pushed outward with my right foot to spin the board round-and-round with my heel. Couldn't do it. *Damnit, try again.* This time landed on the wheels. *Damnit, try again!* Now landed edgewise on the board as I lost my balance and crumpled right on my ass straight on the ground. *This isn't fun.* I glanced over at Donnie, whizzing back and forth all over the place as if it were no one's business. I stood there, panting, trying to get my wind back, before I focused on more remedial ollies over the sidewalk cracks. Well, maybe I wasn't a good skateboarder, but at least I wasn't a poser.

A couple hours later, sweat-soaked and spent, Donnie and I caught the bus back to his row house in Lawrenceville, our skateboards in tow. I called Mom and let her know I was ready to be picked up. Donnie and I plopped ourselves on the couch to watch the boob tube while gulping down mugs of sugary sweet root beer. The ten o'clock news was halfway through when I noticed through the front window a pair of car headlights slowing to stop just outside Donnie's front porch. Sad, but knowing that duty still called, I grinned "later, dude" as I left the land of my fun friend to recede back into the folds of family.

*****

The following Sunday morning…

…renewed the onslaught of demands placed on me despite last night's respite. Indeed, it would not have been so serious if Sunday afternoons or evenings were at issue. But the clock on my schedule started ticking from very early in the morning. No less than as if it were a school day, 7:30 AM was the latest I could arise before evoking parental ire. Again, the hot shower that could have lasted five hours was a mere five minutes, pulling myself into ill-fitting clothes, hurriedly downing a bowl of floating cold cereal for breakfast, collecting my spiral notebooks and study materials, then trying to pull out of a mental haze on the ride there.

But our destination wasn't church. You must understand, my father was a PhD and my mother was an MBA. Religion, or at least organized religion, got short shrift in this household. We didn't even have a copy of the Bible in our house. But it wasn't just my parents who disliked church; it was we kids, too. Whenever Mom and Dad sent Justin and me to Central Christian Presbyterian, either to make us believers or to just socialize with the kids, we two would howl and scream our displeasure the whole way there. Church sermons were boring and interminable, their messages Pollyannaish or Jeremiah-ish. The guy kids were punchy bullies, the girls ugly and mean. For whatever reason, my parents didn't push church on me. That strikes me as odd, because the entire Korean community in all of Pittsburgh was sure to be at that one single location every Sunday morning, and the peer pressure must have been enormous.

But anyways, forget about church! Our destination was White Oak, Pennsylvania, a diminutive middle-class neighborhood where the wizened widower Mrs. Martha resided in an unassuming red-brick colonial. She was an English SAT tutor that Justin and I were chauffeured off to by Mom for consecutive one-on-one lessons, drilling antonyms, testing reading comprehension, and running through analogies in mind-numbing prep for the Scholastic Aptitude Test.

"OK Jay, please give me an antonym for 'ambiguous,'" Mrs. Martha began in a round, bright warble, her right hand almost imperceptibly shaking despite her grip on a pen. I couldn't help but notice how frail she looked at her advanced age, but she still had all her marbles.

As for me, I sat down in a stiff wooden armchair, on the opposite side of a small particleboard laminated and steel legged table, as I constantly shifted between placing my arms on the rests and dropping them into my lap. I nervously kept changing my mind.

"How about 'clear'?" I offered tentatively, feeling somewhat unnerved to be under the gun. I fidgeted under the table, my hands clasped in my lap, twiddling my thumbs.

"Very good." *Wow, dodged a bullet there…* "Now then, how about the word 'arbitrary'? Can you give me the three definitions of 'arbitrary' that I taught you last week?" She laid her veiny hand flat on her side of the table to calm the shaking. While her face was wrinkled and her build was slight, there was something vaguely menacing about her, as if she knew things I didn't. *How can I tell her three definitions if I don't even know one?*

I was clueless. I had completely forgotten, and now there was nowhere to hide. What was I going to do? I felt like a contestant on a TV game show who doesn't know the answer to the million-dollar question: completely put on the spot, his ignorance on display for all to see.

"I think one of the definitions is 'helpful,' right?" I offered timidly. I knew I was wrong; I was just shooting in the dark. A gray pall of glum sullenness settled over me.

"No Jay, as we discussed earlier, the word 'arbitrary' means three things: random, tyrannical, and capricious," Mrs. Martha answered stridently, as if she had something over me, but also as if she were supremely disappointed in me. *What a guilt trip!*

"Jay, I think we need to practice the definition of 'arbitrary' again for next week, until you get it right. I would like you to study the word's three meanings until we meet again." *Damnit, more work!*

"Yes, ma'am," I smiled painfully, hiding hurt and humiliation, and unhappy at the prospect of repeating the lesson.

"OK, Jay," Mrs. Martha quipped, as she wrote some figures in her old-fashioned spiral notebook, her handwriting a chickenscratch scrawl, what with her shaky hands and uncontrollable pen grip. "That concludes our lesson. I will see you next Sunday, same time."

"Thank you, ma'am," I replied, feebly expressing my gratitude as I turned to get out of that stiff wooden chair.

I opened the door and walked out into the rather bourgeois living room, where my mother and Justin waited for me to finish my lesson.

"Everything OK?" Mom asked querulously.

“Yes, everything’s fine,” I lied with a pensive smile, inwardly downcast and grouchy. But how arbitrary of Mrs. Martha!

*****

That Sunday evening…

“Jay! Justin! Come and eat! *Yobo! Bap mok ja!*”

Justin and I had received our semester report cards on Friday, but Mom and Dad needed until Sunday to “strategize” and present a “unified front” against us kids. But there was a sign ahead of time: she had prepared a sumptuous and lavish dinner for the family. Cooking was her way of saying, “I love you.” On most other nights, you name it, she made it—Italian lasagna, pizza or spaghetti, American meatloaf or chicken wings, Chinese fried rice or Indian curry rice. She liked to mix it up and concoct a dish for dinner from a different part of the world. But on this special night, the smell of Korean beef *galbi*, bone-in, dark brown, tender and juicy, perfectly marinated with sesame seeds and onions, wafted through the entire house. And there was the *chigae* stew, heaping with potatoes, zucchini, green onions, and white tofu squares in an orange-yellow soybean paste broth. The *chigae* came out in single-serving porcelain bowls, expertly ladled by Mom. The *galbi* was magnificently presented on a white oval serving dish. All of this came with heaps of steaming white rice in a deep bowl, which would be passed around, along with plenty of Korean side dishes, or *banchan*, placed in the middle of the wooden dining room table: spicy red *kimchi* for Dad, marinated anchovies for Justin, salted pollock roe in sesame oil for me, soybean sprouts for Mom, and enough piles of seaweed laver to go around for everybody. The place mats were neatly set, napkins were sharply folded, water glasses beaded droplets on the outside and stood full of floating ice on the inside, chopsticks and spoons were lined up properly, and everything was golden.

But was this so we would feel properly rewarded, or because we were to be fattened for slaughter? That depended on whether I had all A's or one B. There were only those two possibilities, no others. I stopped tickling the family Steinway Model L's ivories and beat out my brother who bounded up the stairs in a race to the dining-room dinner table. The family sedan had pulled into the driveway only a few minutes earlier, and Dad's commute after another Sunday at the office had whipped up his appetite, legendary among his colleagues at dinner parties. All four of us soon plunked ourselves down in the dining room at the wooden table. As we settled in, the lights hung down over the table and gave off a yellowish sunny glow, quite a contrast to the harsh darkness of an early evening Pittsburgh winter outside.

We strained to attack the hot servings, but of course Dad always got to go first. He inquired about my day and Justin's day as he piled a good half of the steaming rice onto his plate.

"Dad, here, look at this!" I said excitedly, presenting as an offering the most recently issued, unalterable and non-returnable report card for parental inspection.

His mouth full of food, Dad would react to the usual all-A's in the following way: "Hmm. Hmm-mm. Good job, Jay! All A's! That's what I like to see! Keep it up! I'm proud of you!" Then he would hand the report card to Mom for safekeeping. This was contrived cheerleading, of course. I felt deeply rewarded but also somewhat patronized by Dad's congratulatory back-patting.

But that was a better reception than the one for my rarer one-B report card, which would elicit a different reaction: "OK, one B. Now Jay, I know you're better than that. Make sure you get rid of that B next time. You know you can maintain all-A's, right? Just work harder!" Then sadness would descend upon me at the dinner table, cruelly extinguishing my appetite, making me forget food, forcing me to sit there listlessly, statue-like. But, unable at that age to verbalize what I was feeling, I would simply make an effort to put a chicken wing to my lips and nibble on it.

And so the evening's main event concluded with my being reminded and motivated to keep my eyes on the prize: Harvard was "highly recommended," while Yale was "remedially acceptable." Dinner would almost always end in under 30-minutes flat, until we ravenous vultures left behind only bare bones piled up on messy dishes like an animal's skeletal corpse, or only flecks of sauce that were not worth our attention. So we would go our separate ways; I would hit the books, Justin would squeak the cello, Dad would pore over his research articles, and without fail, Mom would balance the heaping stack of dirty, heavy dishes straight to the kitchen, like Sisyphus and his boulder. And so dinner would come and go, just like that.

CHAPTER TWO

PARK YOUR CAR IN HARVARD YARD

Dad and I were about to go for a ride. It was an early Saturday morning in September 1993, around 6 AM, and the new fall sun was already out, shining through the trees of the forest, alighting on the frost heavy on the grass. We were aiming for an E.T.A. of around dinnertime. The grey family station wagon was finally loaded and filled to the brim with laundry baskets and suitcases, and I was receiving a singular send-off. Mom and Grandma sobbed their goodbyes and hugged me over and over again as if I were a P.O.W. being carted off by the North Korean Reds to a Siberian gulag, never to be heard from again. No tears dripped from my eyes. I couldn't figure out what could possibly be the hubbub. I wasn't being executed or kidnapped. And I'd be back during the summer and winter breaks. I was happy to be able to escape into the passenger seat of the station wagon, and I wiggled myself in across from Dad who had taken the driver's seat.

But I realized that this was a big farewell for Mom and Grandma. They were seeing their first (grand) son in the family go off to bigger and better things. How could it not be a momentous occasion? Besides, it was indeed sad, because I was heading from innocent childhood to full adulthood, and no one could reverse the ripening of a green apple. I just couldn't see it that way at the time, that day, since I saw things from the perspective of a young man.

"So, are you ready Jay?" Dad smiled over at me as we fastened our seat belts.

"Yeah, let's go," I replied, still mystified by Mom and Grandma's display of emotion.

We crawled out of the house driveway, turned around in the cul-de-sac, and began its long journey to New England. Mom and Grandma receded in the rearview mirror and then we were off, with our sights set on the road in front of us. *So I'm legally an adult now...so I'll be living away from home...So I'm leaving for Harvard...So I'm about to exert my brain in ways it has never been exerted before...Hold on, this is a HUGE deal!*

But nothing much happened during that drive. For almost the entire car ride, from six in the morning to six in the evening, from Pittsburgh to Cambridge, nothing substantial was said at a point in time when the conversation might have been overflowing. We mostly sat through a strange, awkward silence, occasionally punctuated by mundane remarks about gas stations and restroom stops, although I was bursting with things to say, things full of meaning just below the surface. But it was an awkwardness that I had learned to get used to, and I knew that I would need to figure things out on my own from this point forward.

*****

As we finally arrived at our destination, I peered out the passenger window of the station wagon. We inched into the driveway entrance of an iron-gated yard full of red-brick Colonial architecture. There were cars with open backdoors and pulled up rear trunks everywhere. All makes and models, of all colors of the rainbow, some positioned neatly on the asphalt, others sprawled carelessly on the grass. I spotted Weld Hall from the map, while, after determined and sustained effort, Dad found a miracle parking spot as the September sun set with its glowing rays.

"Alright, let's go!" Dad shouted in that entrepreneurial spirit of his, as he opened the driver's side car door. I silently hauled myself out on the passenger side.

"OK, so Weld fifth floor, Room 52," I said as I showed the map to Dad.

He and I each took a laundry basket full of clothes and a suitcase or backpack, and then Dad locked the car. We headed to my designated red-brick newly renovated dormitory and its bright lamplights on the blue-painted first floor. We took the elevator to the fifth floor and turned down the hall to Weld 52.

The fifth floor was the highest, so the ceiling peaked in the middle and the windows revealed an eye-catching view of the interior of the Yard, although you had to peek a little bit through the branches of the nearby trees. Everything about my suite spelled "N-E-W." The un-creaky parquet floors had recently been laminated, a sheet-white coat of paint covered all four walls, the fluorescent lights brilliantly shined down from the ceiling, and the birch furniture showed no scuff marks nor any engraved "John loves Jane" graffiti. In other words, a fresh start!

Dad really took charge now. He identified a two-person bedroom within the suite and claimed it for me. "OK, now let's unpack," he directed and we began the process of placing clothes in drawers and knick-knacks on drawer tops.

After 15 minutes of this uninteresting activity, I took a break and sat on the edge of one of the unoccupied beds. I was feeling that familiar "dolorous haze" descend and blanket my entire existence, immobilizing me.

Observing me and now concerned, Dad encouraged me to branch out on my own:

"Alright, Jay, the rest you do. I'm not going to do it for you."

"OK, Dad," I mumbled, feeling dejected, anxious and disturbed by my new surroundings.

I followed my father out of the suite to the car. There we hugged and offered each other a final farewell, a strangely intimate ending to an emotionally distant journey. I watched him get in the station wagon and back up before slowly exiting the Yard, taking a right turn around the corner and disappearing out of sight, but not out of mind, nor out of heart.

*****

With Dad gone, I ventured to meet my roommates. Adam, a white guy of slight build, wore straight-leg jeans and a tucked-in flannel collared shirt; he sort of looked like Seinfeld. He had a mullet in the back, at a time when mullets were still popular as a vestige of late 80's haircuts. We met each other just outside his room, in the hallway.

"What's up, man, I'm Adam. Did you just get in?" We shook hands, both of us smiling at the other, although I was miffed about his commandeering the sole single bedroom to himself.

"Hi, I'm Jay. Nice to meet you. I got in after you did, so I took the second available room," I responded, hinting at my slight dismay. His smile froze. "When did you get in?" I continued.

"Oh, a couple hours ago. I think we really lucked out with Weld, don't you think?"

"Yeah, I'd have to say. I'm glad to be here!" I was getting tired of the mundane conversation, and I think Adam sensed it in my body language, as I started turning sideways, as if poised to turn the other way.

"Oh sorry, man, my mom's helping with my move-in." He went to clasp my hand again. "I gotta go help her, so I'll talk to you later, alright?"

My bullshit meter went up, *ting!* right then. There was something about that brief conversation that was on one hand, very instrumental and political, and on the other hand, rather insubstantial and superficial. I suppose I didn't like the way Adam dismissively waved off the conversation toward the end, although I suppose I gave him some pretext to do so. I also realized he was one of those people who could carry on a conversation about absolutely nothing at all, although I suppose a little small talk never hurt anybody. Getting bad vibes, I shook my head and looked askance at him as he walked away.

As I returned to the common room of Weld 52, Smurfy openly and amiably greeted me—another white guy. He was a self-styled southern gentleman from South Carolina's Governor's School for the Gifted. OK, so far, so good. Hmm, I had never seen anybody wearing a black vest with matching black fedora, with black jeans and black tennis shoes, with apparently a black leather belt, too, against a white buttoned shirt, the only piece of clothing that was not black on him. Still, no red flags went up inside of me. In excitement, Smurfy walked me over to his prized possession, a six-foot high plastic tower display containing every single Depeche Mode CD known to man, albums as well as singles, from oldest to most recent, popular or obscure, and that's when I registered quiet alarm in the back of my mind. I mean, a few CDs here and there I can understand, but hundreds dedicated to just one band? That's a little weird…

As I slowly backed away, Smurfy seemed to pick up on my alarm, and became upset. "See there, Jay? You started speaking more slowly to me after I told you I was from the Deep South, as if I'm retarded!"

"What? I mean, what? I did?" I asked, totally taken aback, and now backing up faster.

"Yes, you did!" he insisted.

I disentangled myself from the conversation with a hurried excuse, and scurried back into my room, ostensibly to unpack but really to just get out of that conversational dead-end.

Phil came by an hour later. He was a skinny and short Italian American who didn't like ethnic food. A week or so after move-in, we Asians on the floor treated him to a sushi lunch. Phil totally mangled his portion, complaining loudly and bitterly while disassembling a tuna roll.

"What is this shit?" he griped. "I can't eat this. Who would eat something like this? It's disgusting!"

At the same sushi lunch, Smurfy egged on Phil (*Just try it, OK? Try something different!*), while he himself could barely stomach a salmon roe roll, and washed it down with a generous swig of Coca-Cola. Smurfy, with his 5'6" frame and Napoleon complex, had been demonstrating a consistent habit of being confrontational with Phil, his own roommate.

On that first day, Jerseyboy showed up last with his hovering Chinese parents and a high-pitched effeminate-sounding voice, and after us roommates had begun to know each other for a while, we all began to wonder behind his back if he was ever teased or bullied in high school about it.

“Oh my GAWD, Jay, it’s SO nice to finally meet you, how ARE you doing?” Jerseyboy would go on in a super-enthusiastic voice, with a huge affected smile on his face, eyes squinting into crescent moons. But as his roommate, I knew that he didn’t have a single gay bone in his body, for the single fact that he kept bringing girls into our bedroom. First it was the high school girlfriend he broke up with shortly after his arrival at Harvard, then Katie whom he dated for three years in college, and then finally Rachel his senior year sweetheart. Let’s face it, that guy got more chicks than any of us in the room ever did.

As for the rest of Weld’s fifth floor, the only thing that united us all was our gender; there were no coeducational floors. The one individual I got to know well was Kee, a Korean-American originally from Buffalo, New York, who lived two doors down the hall in Weld 54. Kee was short and stocky but had a degree of personality finesse. He liked playing the clarinet in a classical orchestra as much as jumping into the mosh pit at a Mighty Mighty Bosstones concert. Together we would make the trek in the cold autumn morning every week that freshman fall to the Harvard-Yenching Library for Elementary Korean, a class that we alternately scorned and adored as an inside joke, one that was "highly recommended" by both our fathers. Out of everybody on Weld's fifth floor, only he knew as well as I did the sort of authoritarian parenting and prodding we had endured as Korean first sons.

*****

Classes came right out of the bend, and soon I and all my 1,599 other freshmen classmates were walloped by the intensity. Since we did not have to declare a "concentration" (which is a "major" at every other college campus) until the end of freshman year, we could afford to be experimental in our choice of classes for a couple semesters.

Multivariable calculus in the fall seemed like a sure bet because I had been good with numbers in high school. In fact, Phil and I took the class together for moral support and because we were cocky enough to believe we would be fine grade-wise if working as a team. Yet soon it became apparent to us that no matter how hard we applied ourselves, some of our classmates were mathematical geniuses. *What? Phil and I scored a*

70 on a simple pop quiz, while somebody broke the curve? Oh my God, no! I figured out in a hurry that my high school did not train me as well as Bedford-Stuyvesant or Exeter trained their students. The tables had been turned: whereas before I had been the math god in high school, now I was the mere mortal at Harvard.

"Jay, let's hire a tutor, because we're getting blown away!" Paul yelped, as we went over the results of the midterm exam with growing alarm. And that's exactly what we did—hire a tutor—because we were going the wrong way, with percentages heading south and grades going down.

Our first meeting with the tutor was a lesson in ego-destruction. We felt like little kids sitting in the classroom corner with conehead dunce caps on our skulls. The tutor relayed to us, slowly and methodically, as if we were retards, "OK, Paul, Jay, when you find the derivative of x, it's important to remember that the corresponding integral is…"

Wait, didn't I cover this stuff in high school and score a perfect 5 on the AP Math Exam? But this was college-level multivariable calculus, not the watered down high school rotgut. So after ceaseless anxious effort, we worked with the tutor to get our grades up to a flat B as a final semester mark. But knowing now that I had no competitive advantage in any field remotely mathematical, I gave that route up. Indeed, in many subjects, I found out much to my dismay that I was the typical "average brilliant student" at Harvard, a dubious distinction that I just couldn't manage to shake.

But—and this was a big exception—there was one class in this whole intellectual enterprise that I eventually settled down with, and which I didn't even from the beginning consider as a possible concentration: "Introduction to Ancient Greek Philosophy," taught by Professor Susan. Right away, one thing worked to my advantage: all words, no numbers. Looking back, I essentially enrolled in an obscure little class to read strange esoteric material that I had little background on, prior knowledge of, or training in. But the course catalogue explained the importance of philosophy to me, that it was the ancient core of the modern university, that philosophical texts are some of the oldest texts we possess, and that philosophy superseded all the specialized disciplines located in today's academy. And most important, I was genuinely interested in philosophy, enough so that despite the freezing chill of winter in Cambridge, which made getting up for a 9 AM morning class seem impossible, I managed to get there early every time. My boots would crunch through the stiff, crackly frost on the permanently green grass, as I took shortcuts instead of staying on the concrete pathways formally patterned throughout the Yard. My oversized parka shrouded my rail-thin frame, insulated in blue jeans, flannel shirt, and bulky wool sweater.

Once in the classroom, after we students shrugged off the layers of outerwear to settle in our flip-folding lecture hall chairs, Professor Susan would begin with a few introductory words. "As you know from our last meeting, philosopher Sextus Empiricus provides us with a tattered fragment of secondary commentary on Anaximander's cosmogony…" I knew what she was talking about, because I was diligent with the readings. This was about the pre-Socratics, or the Greek philosophers before the time of Plato and Socrates. Right away, the "meaning of life," as popularly attributed to be the sole concern of philosophy, was being taken with rock-solid seriousness as a subject of pressing and urgent importance.

*****

Writing the final term paper at Weld 52 for Professor Susan's class turned out to be an enjoyable intellectual exercise. I just saw it as writing out some common-sense thinking. In my five-pager on Aristotle's Physics, I retraced the argument from the beginning about the biological nature and social behavior of animate beings, whether human beings or animals, and the nature of their causes to change or move. I actually made a point of finding fault with Aristotle's line of argument, challenging his conclusions and daring to replace them with my own. I just called it as I saw it, as my common-sense versus Aristotle's common sense, but apparently it raised eyebrows because Professor Susan summoned me to her office.

I had to pick up my graded paper, but I was worried about getting chewed out for gross insubordination. Professor Susan's office was soberly decorated, with the black speckled linoleum outside her office transitioning through the wooden door's entrance into grey-brown carpet with innumerable books lining the bookshelves attached to the whitewashed walls. The only thing high-tech was the computer on her wooden desk. Professor Susan herself was dressed in a flowing dark grey blouse with matching long dark grey skirt that partially hid her black oxford shoes. She wore a kind and ready smile, and her hair was cut short and cropped close.

"Jay, oh…hi, come on in!" was her enthusiastic and warm greeting.

"Hi Professor, how are you?" I replied, a little shyly.

"I'm fine, young man. I read your paper. Look here," she directed, flipping the pages. "What you have here is a conflation. Aristotle does not say what you thought he said. But otherwise, you did a very good job." On the paper was a B+. There was no grade inflation here, but at least I didn't need a tutor.

"Oh, I see." I was trying hard to see her argument.

"You're a freshman, right?"

"Yes, Professor," I replied, politely receptive to her query.

"You really do have it, you do. Have you declared your concentration yet?"

"I don't have a concentration yet," I told her as I started to panic inside.

"Here, let me show you something," Professor Susan said, while she reached for a slim, small volume on the library shelf in her office. She then opened it up to show me a page. It was a Platonic dialogue, in the original Greek. *Whoa, this is cool!* "See? If you learn Greek, you too can also read the Platonic dialogues in the original language," she offered positively.

"Wow, Professor… that's fascinating." That calmed me down right away, as I looked back up and matched her smiling gaze.

"So I think you should declare your concentration in philosophy."

"Really, Professor?"

"Yes, I do!"

My panic subsiding completely, I then excused myself after this hearty embellishment to my self-esteem. Indeed, Introduction to Ancient Greek Philosophy was my favorite course that freshman year altogether. After that realization, I decided that concentrating in philosophy would make sense. So I made my way to the Administrative Office on the third floor of Emerson Hall to formally petition the Department to make philosophy my concentration. I felt elated, relieved and unbelievably lucky, too, that things had worked out for me up to this point.

*****

One hurdle on the road to declaring philosophy my concentration was clearing it with my parents. I thought Dad would be particularly curious about what educational choices I made that determined how his money was being spent. A few days after meeting with Professor Susan and finalizing the formal petition to concentrate in philosophy, I made what I thought would be a difficult phone conversation with the Old Man and Momma. Truth be told, it wasn't a hard sell at all, but a walk in the park!

"So what is your major now, Jay?" Mom and Dad both asked quizzically, each one echoing the other over the phone.

I began, "Well, I chose philosophy finally," as I hastened to add, out of fear of needing to please them, "because philosophy trains you in critically analyzing readings, identifying lines of arguments in texts, verbalizing written points of view, boiling complex information down to a few simple propositions, all skills that can be applied to just about any profession, but specifically to the law..." It was as if I were recounting a laundry list.

"OK, Jay, OK, that's fine, so you want to be a lawyer, eh?" and to that my Dad was generally approving of the idea that I wanted, despite my heavy liberal arts emphasis, to be a bourgeois professional one day, and not some crazy countercultural hippie goner. I suppose that if I had chosen Women's Studies or Archaeology, they would have been genuinely worried, but this time, there was no concerned quibbling from Mom, no second-guessing by Dad. After the phone conversation, I noted deep down to myself how I still needed to please my parents with all sorts of self-justifications.

But there was something surprisingly noncommittal or hands-off about their attitude on that phone call, almost a certain apathy or listlessness in their tone of voice. In a remarkably enlightened manner for first-generation Korean immigrant parents, they felt the importance of treating me like an adult once I entered college, and perhaps they genuinely felt that they needed to ease up on me a bit. Maybe it was the sinking realization that they no longer had any control over my interests, that starting from age 18, it was the beginning of the end of my time with them, and that I would need to look onward and forward.

Years ago, in the prime of my adolescence, Dad, driving the family car, had once said on the way back from a satisfying restaurant dinner out on the town, with everyone in the family inside the car as witnesses, "Once you reach the age of 18, Jay, you can do whatever you want." I was captivated: *really? Whatever I want?* Well, if I could vote for President, if I could fight and die for my country, I could at least also choose my college major. Now that freedom had at last come true. I really was on my own now, and the feeling was, well...rather new.

And so, although my parents never contested my choice of major and gave me that freedom, it was still important for me not to be derelict in my duty as a responsible son, one faithful to his studies and unfailing in effort, just as my father himself had unflinchingly upheld his duty as a responsible father to support his son's education with flagging.

*****

Of course, we freshmen all had to blow off steam, so again I pursued sports and music. I signed up for freshmen lacrosse, hoping to get a grip on my anger issues. We were the most lackadaisical outfit you could imagine. We would sit there listlessly on the grass in the preternaturally hot April sun, making small talk, after a few half-hearted man-ball drills and passing/shooting practice. We were such a bunch of jag-offs; we just didn't care. And we were just having too much fun hanging out than being oh-so-boringly competitive.

Of course, as you would expect, it didn't matter what happened in the games—as a team we were so hilariously bad—but what transpired outside. One time, right before we took the field against the season's toughest opponent, a scrappy bunch from a public university with many ethnic minority players, our coach huddled us together.

"Look guys, we're going to lose, so just forget about what happens today," he advised. "But remember, in five years, these guys will be pumping gas into each of your ten BMWs!"

I involuntarily laughed out loud, because already back in those days, by then, public discourse had become stultifyingly politically correct, so it was refreshing to hear someone just speak their mind. Yet I had been one of those public-school minority have-nots on the other side, just as now I was one of the privileged Harvard haves, so while I appreciated Coach's candor, I couldn't say I shared his views. I still remembered the stinging sensation of feeling like an outsider, an underdog, one of the unclubbables. It didn't sit well with me. In fact, underneath it all I supposed I was shocked and offended by Coach's comment. Still, I set a precedent with my humorous reaction, because some of my white prep school teammates also joined in and laughed good-naturedly, relieved that I wasn't going to stick it to them for enjoying some light humor.

During practice, we had set up two goals to simulate a full-size playing field. That day the women's lacrosse team needed one for their practice, so their coach approached ours, who acquiesced pleasantly to her face. But behind her back, as he returned to us, he directed gruffly: "Hey guys, put back one of the goals for the ladies. And hurry up before we have another Feminist Revolution on our hands…!"

Again, I chortled, because as a man I could see the humor from our shared point of view. But still, many strong-willed women had actively taken part in my adolescent education: Mrs. Martha the English tutor, Mrs. Li my piano teacher, and my own mother, as well as Professor Susan, all whom I had come to respect and admire. So I laughed, and so did my teammates, but I in fact felt unsure about my own reaction, because the joke was ultimately making light of a serious issue.

After every practice, the guys would head back to the gym and wind down from the activities of the previous hour or so with a group shower. With the exception of me, everybody would fling their clothes off and prance into the main room, completely naked from head to toe, with nothing other than a washcloth, and jump around, hooting and hollering, slapping each other's asses, high-fiving, with the multiple shower faucets blasting hot steaming water right and left. Feeling this was too homoerotic for my tastes, I would shake my head and make the long trek back to Weld Hall and take my own individual shower. At least no one seemed to mind.

I parted ways with lacrosse after that season, despite the fun and relaxed nature of this freshman-level team. I didn't even go to the end-of-season party, although I was warmly invited, and I knew hilarity would ensue. Let's face it: I didn't go to a top boarding school; my mother wasn't from old money; my father wasn't a Senator or a CEO; and most important, as a player, I wasn't a standout. My on-the-fly stick skills on offense were average at best, and at my weight, I wasn't an effective enforcer on defense. I had also heard stories about graduating to Junior Varsity lacrosse, supposedly a lot more hard work and not nearly as much fun. And that was to say absolutely nothing of Varsity lacrosse. Besides, nobody on the team took our coach seriously, who set a bad example; he was a classic case of what not to do as a leader. Mind you, I didn't have anything personally against him, and perhaps underneath it all I was actually quite fond of him, because he spoke his mind. But overtly sexist and racist comments ultimately didn't fly in my book.

Music also diverted my attention, but I no longer was a performance artist in classical music. I explored the avenues on that one, and they were all closed. There was an air of pretentiousness among the classical musicians at Harvard that was astounding, to put it mildly. These people obviously thought very highly of themselves in a way that made them unapproachable. Another problem was that pianists didn't audition for solo recitals but for concertos with orchestra, and I didn't have an advantage there, since the only one I knew was the first movement of Edvard Grieg's Piano Concert in A Minor. Finally, the vetting process was very competitive, very opaque and very political. Instead of just being genuinely interested in the subject matter, or being highly talented on an instrument, kissing certain people's asses was required to be a part of this exclusive cult of personality. I didn't need that. I just threw my hands up and walked away.

What appealed to me instead as an exploratory alternative, as I rounded the folding tables set up on the Harvard Yard lawn for student groups hawking their wares to freshmen, was a position for a Jazz DJ of WHRB-95.3 FM Harvard Radio. The representative that day was immensely kind and very receptive to my questions. He told me that my lack of knowledge about jazz music was not a problem; you just got better while you learned on the job. And finally, he didn't demand me to kiss his ass. It seemed the kind of thing that would suit my personality, very egalitarian and no bullshit.

I was awarded my Federal Communications Commission license by passing a test of the studio equipment and paying a small fee. The station housed a wonderfully vast collection of aging but serviceable LPs, as well as a growing library of CDs and a respectable vault of cassette tapes which I could delve into and explore. It was a bit tricky, alternating between the two turntables while syncing levels on the 18-track mixer, all the while working the pair of CD players and recording sessions with a double cassette tape-player. I also oversaw the two phone lines and I emceed the live microphone. The first selection I ever played was Miles Davis's "Kind of Blue," which, interestingly, described exactly how I felt. I must have played that tune a hundred times that academic year.

*****

But neither lacrosse nor WHRB could keep me on the straight and narrow. I and my roommates raged in other ways. On typical Friday nights, we traveled down the main road towards the Charles River to The Grille. The secret to getting into The Grille was possession of a fake

ID; even a flimsily constructed one would grant you access. We freshmen would proceed *en masse* in the direction of this watering hole, and fortunately the weather was still mild in September, because if you tried to make your way back in January too sauced, you might actually collapse on the sidewalk and freeze to death.

The Grille was an unassuming place, with a jukebox in the corner, a bar on one side, mirrors around and around to check one's self out, some rudimentary wooden booths set up opposite the bar, and a hallway which led in the back to the primitive restrooms, the men's of which usually had at least one urinal overflowing with someone's puke. It wasn't a dancing crowd, but we would mill around like a school of fish while we drank like fish. I too would drink myself sick on sweet cider and avoid conversation, because converting the sad sobriety inside of me to happy inebriation on the outside required laser-focused attention.

But unlike access to alcohol from the Grille, which partially masked my sadness, I couldn't find a source for pot, to take the edge off my anger. Freshman lacrosse had served that purpose for one freshman semester, but not the next one. One weekend night, Phil the sushi-hater and Smurfy the Depeche Mode lover, who were still technically bunkmates, got into a heated argument over what exactly I have long since forgotten. It was a classic conflict, both of them compensating for their short and skinny statures, one mild-mannered but now ruffled, the other acerbic and now expressing it, one conservative, the other liberal, and both sharing the same cramped space. After this hissy-fit, the two demanded that I take sides, which I did.

Enraged, Phil pointed fingers. "Jay, why are you taking sides with Smurfy? I thought you were my FRIEND!"

I was initially dumbfounded. No one had ever asked me before to take sides in a war between two friends. To this I replied, unnecessarily escalating the conflict, "Phil, what was I supposed to do? Smurfy had a point, so I just called it as I saw it! You're completely out of line, man! If you cross me again like that, I'll kick your fucking ass!" I was screaming, completely unbalanced and totally irrational, as if someone had unloosed a screw in my emotional hardwiring and had thrown a monkey wrench into the works. Talk about labile mood, with slow return to baseline! I panted like a greyhound that had just chased the rabbit around the track. Clearly, something was wrong with me. I really needed that weed to chill me out.

*****

One day after classes, I sensed heightened excitement in the suite. It was April 1994, and the buzz was about the so-called lottery of freshman rooming groups into one of the dozen or so upperclassmen "Houses," otherwise known as "dormitories" on nearly any other college campus. Most Houses had a distinctive character to it.

Adams House was traditionally the artsy-fartsy house, where writers and poets engaged in excessive coffee-drinking and cigarette-smoking. Mather House was the quintessential jock house, replete with beer bonging, keg stands, and casual sex. House membership had become randomized through a lottery selection process so that the distinctive character of each House had been diluted somewhat, but there were still vestiges of the old traditions. The artist-poets stranded in other Houses would still make the trip to be with the aesthetes in residence in Adams House, while the soccer and field hockey players marooned in other Houses would make the extra effort to party with fellow athletes in Mather House. The one exception was the Quad, containing three Houses geographically isolated in the northern-most section of campus, all of which had no specific tradition, and thus registered no real attractiveness.

My rooming group had materialized after a couple weeks of tense deliberation and urgent politicking. Jerseyboy and I had more than a couple extended discussions while we lay in our respective beds in the dark, about whether we should take Phil or Smurfy. We had already chosen Kee, even though he was located down the hall, because he was Asian and generally agreeable. But we needed four to make an even group. We liked Phil because he was generally mild-mannered, tidy in personal habits, and conscientious. We didn't like Smurfy because he was argumentative, had poor hygiene and could be neurotic. It seemed like a no-brainer. But ultimately we went with Smurfy, not for any of the reasons stated above, but because he leaned liberal and was open to differences. We couldn't forgive Phil for openly destroying his sushi lunch at the restaurant, while Smurfy had devoured the food at least with feigned relish. And I had a nagging feeling about the verbal altercation I had had with Phil…what if it happened again? Yeah, Smurfy could be nasty, too, but I could handle his irritability. Phil on the other hand had somehow managed to pick me apart emotionally. I talked about this with Jerseyboy in secret, and with each of us supporting the other, we approached Weld 52's only citizen from the South.

"Smurfy, we'd like to have you in our upperclassmen rooming group," I told him, with Jerseyboy smiling in agreement, backing me up.

"Thanks guys, I knew you'd do the right thing," he replied haughtily.

Jerseyboy and I almost reversed our decision right there at that moment. It wasn't the first time that Smurfy came that close to getting his ass kicked.

Soon after that, the Floor Tutor called everybody on Weld's fifth to his room. He carried small white envelopes in his hand, and announced that House rooming decisions had been made: "Smurfy, Jay, Jerseyboy and Kee, over here…!" Smurfy commandeered the initiative and grabbed for the card to open it, as we three Asians hovered around and circled around the token white guy.

"Please, let it be a good one!" Jerseyboy squealed in his gay, high-pitched voice.

"Hey, anything but the Quad, guys!" I remarked, trying to spin the situation in the best light.

"Just give me a quiet room," Kee muttered under his breath.

As Smurfy read the fine print, it was great news. We had placed 26th out of 400 and were selected for Adams House. The four of us all jumped up and down, hugging each other as if we had just won a relay race. How had we lucked out so well? And what's more, our room would be Claverly Hall 5, in a building that was overflow housing for several nearby Houses, including Adams, one floor up with a beautiful balcony containing a fire escape and overlooking the intersection of the National Lampoon, Lowell House and Adams House. We would be left alone, unsupervised and unmonitored, in a building containing a room that had the best strategic vantage point out of any on campus.

Others floating by with their cards examined our paperwork with envy and jealousy. Some got really bad news. Adam and his buddies were placed 325th out of 400, and they were to be sent packing to Cabot House, in the Quad. Adam kept shaking his head in denial, while his roommates wailed their dissatisfaction and unhappiness. Now it was every man for himself. I watched Adam get on the phone and speak quietly but urgently, going back and forth with an administrator to relay his grievances, so that changes could be made to the official decision.

"Hi sir, I believe that my Harvard experience does not include membership in a House in the Quad, so far away from campus life…Yes, er…Yes, sir…I expect equal treatment, and it's unfair to be stuck in Cabot House…" Adam argued, stating his case. Poor guy.

So now, with philosophy as my concentration in the classroom, and Adams House my home-on-campus, the wheels of Fate began to turn. And that is the end of the beginning!

CHAPTER THREE

RAVE ON!

Sophomore year began to take shape party-wise. I tired of the bar scene as a way to pick myself up, and I was getting irritated about the lack of pot to bring me down. Wasn't there a single substance that could do both?

I had been fascinated with the rave scene, although I was too sequestered at home and chained to my studies in Pittsburgh to ever go to one. I found my mental image about raves—the faceless DJ and anonymous partyers congregating at clandestine industrial sites in shady parts of a city metropolis to ingest mind-altering substances and dance all hours of the night to a heavy electronic beat—to be so endlessly exciting and secretively seductive. I was raised on beer and pot in the Western Pennsylvania suburbs and on rock and reggae. Steve

Miller Band was not exactly dance music, nor did Peter Tosh's "Legalize It" incite me to move. And the only shady part of town in Pittsburgh's Fox Chapel was a neighbor's uninsulated basement. Even within Pittsburgh's city limits, the scene was still very provincial. Not much going on in the gateway to the Midwest. But here I was now, right on the Atlantic Seaboard!

So as sophomore year started, my entrance into the rave scene began more or less to fall into place. At Lamont Library, full of dry wooden bookshelves, with a floor drearily linoleum-tiled, housed in a building harshly fluorescent-lit, while all the pre-meds were cramming their chemistry or biology textbooks, I stole away some time to actively pore over a small tome with a purple cover about the history of the street drug XTC. I carefully read and scrutinized every word, every chapter, in that book. *Ah, XTC, huh? Cool name...so much more interesting than biology or chemistry, short for BORING...*

It had apparently first been synthesized in 1912 before World War I by Merck, a respectable German pharmaceutical firm. *Really? By Merck? That long ago?* Then it migrated after World War II to the United States, where it came under the supervision of psychiatrist Dr. Alexander Shulgin in the late 1960s and 1970s as a chemical adjunct to marriage counseling and couples therapy to enhance feelings of empathy and emotional warmth. So it did have a medical use, at least at one time! I also came to realize that in the mid-1980s XTC was criminalized as a Schedule I controlled substance, the most severe level of restriction due to (1) its high potential for abuse, (2) no accepted medical use, and (3) no safe use for the drug. So by 1985 there were stiff penalties for XTC use, whether ostensibly medical or underhandedly recreational. Well, at least I was going into this whole devilish affair with my eyes wide open. *Better not get caught!*

I didn't have a source to buy XTC. Yet I had an inkling that the raves.alt online discussion group was a good bet for that, and would maybe help me get to a rave. I email blasted a post asking for help to get to a rave party, and somebody emailed me back almost immediately:

I can get you to a rave party, if you'd like. BTW, if you need any XTC, let me know. Sam.

I was mystified. *Who is this guy? I don't know him at all!* And yet he apparently went out on a limb to ask me if I wanted to make a business transaction on a Schedule I controlled substance that I was in need of. He could have been a cop, for all I knew, trying to entrap me. I emailed back, making sure not to reveal my full identity or exact location.

Hi, Sam. Yes, I'd like that. Let's meet sometime. I'm in Harvard Square. How about you? Jay

I got his pager number and located his address, which was right on the Harvard campus, and I soon found out that he was a fellow Harvard classmate! Different year, and an anthropology concentrator. And yes, Sam was a real person, too, and no, he was definitely not a cop!

*****

Sam's place was nothing unusual; nothing stood out (and that was the idea, I guess) except a faint odor of pot. When I first met him there, I was struck by how singularly strange he looked, with recessed eyes and albino skin, a hooked nose and pink lips, a shock of unruly white hair, and a tall, skinny body hidden by baggy street clothes. One of Sam's guy friends sat bedside while I plopped myself on the couch and made small talk with this other visitor.

I noticed, conspicuously stacked to the side of Sam's bed, a pile of black covered books. His friend was flipping through one, much to his obvious delight. Sam passed another one on to me. What is this? Wow, thick black markers had left cryptic symbols, not quite numbers or letters, but still filled in with colors. On other pages, there looked to be apparently a word marked down, but surrounded by double-borders and embellishments that made the word incomprehensible, except perhaps to an eye trained to look for specific things.

This was graffiti, or graf for short. Sam's tag name was "Dyrekt," and with that information, it made sense what the symbols on some of the pages spelled out together as a word. I was amazed at this street art: tagging, or bombing, as it were, what Sam and his crew would call putting up graffiti after dark in public yards, on billboards, and on the side of building walls. I wasn't naturally pulled to this "spray can art," so I stayed away from it because I couldn't imagine anything stupider than getting caught for defacing public property. Nevertheless, I admit that the subculture was fascinating as an activity that went alongside rave dancing, illicit drugs and house music.

I noticed something else now as my eyes trained their gaze to the wall above Sam's bed: his CD collection. He didn't have many, but I was interested in his musical preferences.

"So what kind of CDs do you have?" I asked with guarded curiosity.

"Oh, well, I've got dance music CDs, such as DJ Doc Martin mix CDs, hip-hop CDs like Digable Planets, Alkaholiks, Beatnuts…" he trailed off after a while. So, very urban in taste!

I joked, "I'll trade some of my rock and classical CDs for what you got, ha-ha."

We dropped the subjects of music and graffiti and got down to business. From a briefcase hidden under his bed, Sam took out a plastic zip bag with a single round white pill inside, about 3/8" in diameter, scored once on both sides. I made a show of inspecting it and nodded approvingly. *Hell,* I said to myself, *let's give it a try*, out of curiosity, out of a desire for excitement, and out of a need to rid myself of my emotional hang-ups.

"So how much do I owe you?"

"Thirty dollars."

"OK." I reached into my pockets for the bills and offered them to him.

"Thanks, man." Sam took the money and handed me the pill in exchange.

Then the conversation turned to rave parties. He handed me a flyer, a colorful piece of thick paper with the phone number and date and time for the event. The location was secret, to be revealed by calling the listed number on the night of the gathering. Sam offered to score me a ride to this next party he and his friends were going to, called "Casper." I quickly agreed.

So with the girl's eye of Grace, a high school classmate who attended Boston College, to help guide my selections, I went clothes-shopping outside of Cambridge, across the Charles River, on Boston's Commonwealth Avenue, where the interesting and trendy "alternative" shops were. I was so excited to pick out clothes on my own, without the need for parental permission. The street was a novel mix of upper-crust genteel leisure and lowbrow street commerce, where for $40 I could pick up a newsboy "lid" from a hat shop; a pair of baggy jean pants for $55 from an alternative clothing establishment; a pair of flat-soled skate shoes for $80 from a skateboard purveyor; and a plaid patterned quarter-zip front short-sleeve shirt that came in at $45 from a record store that also sold clothes. Naturally, these weren't big sums to anybody living on or near

Commonwealth Avenue, but to the merchants these prices reflected huge markups.

"Hey Grace, does this look good on me?" I asked her like a little girl about one of the pairs of baggy jeans that covered my shoes on the bottom and barely stayed up at the hips.

"Hold on, let me see from the front, sides and back... yeah, it looks good on you," she replied. Whether she told me the truth or not, I'll never know.

"Thanks!" I replied out of naïve reassurance and gratitude.

High fashion, indeed! I had just started working part-time at the Fine Arts Library, so I could bring in a little bit of cash each week, perhaps $50 or $60. This amount I felt comfortable and un-remorseful about spending on drugs, while Mom and Dad would send checks for $100 or $250 every now and then, which I tried to spend only on other sundry miscellaneous items.

*****

October 15, 1994. A day more memorable to me than the day I lost my virginity. It was Saturday night, and the only "rave gear" I had were my clothes, a bottle of water, the XTC pill hidden in the folds of my leather wallet with my ID and a few dollars, and as much charisma and charm as I could muster up, when Sam's ride materialized outside Claverly Hall's front entrance. Two anonymous, generic hatchbacks pulled up, one for the guys, one for the girls, and I was put in with the girls. Why, I'll never know, but I guess it was because there was space.

"Hi! I'm Jessica, Sam's girlfriend," said a white girl sitting in the front passenger seat holding a yellow school-girl backpack in her lap. With her brown hair lit up with bright yellow streaks, she wore a blue polo shirt and a silver skirt with candy-striped leggings—very space-girl cute! She extended her hand to me as I settled on one of the back seats.

"Hey! It's nice to meet you." I reached forward and shook her hand to win her over.

"I'm Holly," said the driver, a white girl wearing dark sunglasses with a black puffy jacket and black baggy jeans offsetting her short blonde hair and white skate-shoes. She extended a hand back past the front seat.

"Hi Holly, what's up? Thanks for the ride." I shook her pale hand briefly so she could return it back to the steering wheel.

"Hey, I'm Jamie." Jamie was sitting next to me in the back seat. She was a red-haired hottie in a solid dark navy and white striped track suit. Her red hair was braided tightly back in one long ponytail. The look she had was a classic, back in those days. She was petite and cute as a button. I automatically felt the heart-panging, butterflies-in-the-stomach feeling I would get whenever I was near an attractive girl. "Here, try this," Jamie suggested, reaching out something in her extended hand. It was opium rolled up in a joint, according to her.

"Well, how can I refuse?" I asked rhetorically.

I admit I was unnerved by the high levels of estrogen in the car. I felt outnumbered and overpowered. But I kept my cool and masked my discomfort with the opium, making sure not to turn down a polite offer unsociably.

We hurtled down the dark highway for an hour without incident, until we reached a small industrial town on the outskirts of metropolitan Boston. The only landmark in sight was a single unassuming building, just red brick and concrete, with drainage pipes trailing down the sides, very nondescript and ugly. Not for a single second did its exterior reveal the hidden world of bright strobe lights, powerful green lasers and huge projector screens housed inside. But you could definitely FEEL and HEAR it: a fast 135 Beats Per Minute thudded away, emanating from the double metal doors and the brick-and-concrete walls, rattling the marrow in your bones.

The asphalt lot outside was another clue as to what was going on inside the building: cars slowly crawled all over, trolling for parking spots, while the parked ones spilled out their human passengers and rave gear cargo. After securing their vehicles, the kids made their way to the line snaking along the side of the building entrance. So this is it!

We emerged out of our two hatchbacks, already drugged and giddy with nervous excitement and ready anticipation. Immediately I felt self-conscious, sized-up, inspected. It was a social setting with all sorts of comparisons being made. The line to get inside displayed a wild diversity of fashions. These teenage and twenty-something kids were children of the hippies, so an "anything goes" 70's-era philosophy blended with a "neo-classical creative" 90's-era Zeitgeist. Every color of the rainbow was represented in the hairstyles, from mauve to burnt umber, platinum to pitch black, yellow in front with blue in the back, and emerald to aquamarine. Piercings went up the ears, little mean hoops pinching the lobes, but also belly button rings for the girls and nose studs for the guys. For lids, there were light or dark baseball caps worn forward and backward, brown or grey apple hats placed front to back, yellow beanies with playful purple tassels and fishing hats with wide brims. For feet, flat-soled skate shoes were common, athletic running shoes did the trick, no high heels anywhere in sight, but three-foot high platform shoes on one enterprising individual (*how did he get around in those?*). For tops, track jackets and baggy sweatshirts were appropriate attire for the guys, while for the girls, halter tops, sports bras and cut-off T-shirts were *de rigeur*, despite the cold. Underneath, skin-tight leather pants and curve-hugging spandex shorts for the girls, and low-riding cargo shorts and super-baggy jeans for the guys completed the look. As far as accessories, I spied twinkling silver purses and shiny gold totes, formal leather slings and casual nylon backpacks, and yes! supercool sunglasses everywhere, despite it being the dead of night.

We finally inched through the entrance. With separate lines for guys and girls, male and female security guards patted us down and went over us with handheld metal detectors that emitted electronic shrieks upon contact with alloy. We offered up our $20 tributes to the Rave God—a diminutive middle-aged man adorned in stonewashed jeans, white tennis shoes and a navy polyester jacket—for safe passage, and as I parted the white bedsheets of a curtain into the darkened main area, I realized it was the start of complete pandemonium.

*****

Alien green lasers shot through the undercover darkness of a sugary-scented machine-made fog blanketing the warehouse space, the spot rented for the night's rave in an industrial neighborhood in Boston. The "four-to-the-floor" house and techno music thudded in my already-overwhelmed ears, increasing from 135 to a constant 140 Beats Per Minute, BOOM! BOOOM!! BOOOOM!!! BOOOOOM!!!! on and on, repeatedly, never-ending, unstoppable, over and over and over again. On the dancefloor, I picked up confusing shadowy glimpses of bodies gyrating to the beat, but I was in absolutely no mood for dancing. It was all I could do to just walk around, feeling like a fish out of water, nervously taking drags off a lit cigarette, trying to calm and contain my anxiety.

As I paced, I peered at and inspected my wristwatch, the time barely visible in the blinking laser lights. In the last half-hour no spiritual awakening had overcome me, nor had any ritual conversion happened to me. I had washed down a quarter of the scored XTC pill 30 minutes ago with a swig of bottled water, then another one-fourth 15 minutes after that with even more *agua*, and yet I still wandered around the tame outskirts of the party, feeling so out-of-place lonely, like the only uninitiated virgin in the entire red-light district of Amsterdam. I flicked my still-lit cigarette butt off into outer space, followed its orange glow down to the floor, and ground it out under my foot before lighting up and chain-smoking another one. I was running out of drugs, out of time, out of water, out of cigarettes, and out of patience…

Admittedly, there was something there, an underlying current of elevated mood, stirring from the depths, as if something were ready to punch through the floor of my ennui and despondence, a muted sign that something was in store for me. I kept walking around the warehouse space, so as to stay busy and not seem like a loser. I had just taken another drag on my cigarette when, from out of nowhere, Sam suddenly appeared.

"Hey, man, I took half and I don't feel anything yet!" I yelled above the noise, starting to wonder if he had sold me short.

But he stood by his goods, yelling back at me: "Just take the rest of it!"

Knowing that he wasn't about to back down, and that I had no leverage over him, in desperate resignation I pulled the remaining half-pill from my wallet and—

down the hatch!—chomped with vengeance on it. I involuntarily retched at the sheer bitterness of its purity, very glad for the last of the bottled water to wash all of the disintegrating particles out of my mouth and down my throat. I tossed the empty plastic bottle off into a corner of the stage, towards the stacks of speakers which emitted painfully loud melodies of fighter-jet sonic booms and the rattling of machine-gun beats.

Now that I had sealed my fate, for better or worse, like it or not, I parked myself off-center on the dancefloor, surrounded by sweaty hot strangers, all by myself in the middle of a crowd. I didn't know where anybody was. I had lost touch with my crew, I had lost touch with my dealer, I was lost, lost, completely and utterly lost...

And then, amidst all the confusion, suddenly I sensed a sharp crack towards the back of my head, as if a wave of white-hot fire were sweeping upward from my medulla and through the layers of wrinkled cerebellum to the enveloping cerebrum, forcing me to suck in air deeply. I squinted inwardly as my brain began to cave in under the pressure, like a galactic supernova collapsing under its own weight, until my gray matter imploded completely under the force and then reverse-exploded outward, radiating white-hot Jesus rays in all directions. I doubled forward to brace myself, hands on knees for support, and held my breath. *Wait, I can't see!*

In my hollow chest, my pounding heart thudded mesmerizingly and at one with the dance rhythm, the very same BOOM! BOOOM!! BOOOOM!!!

BOOOOOM!!!! that had been so unenthralling and out of sync just seconds ago. A wellspring of pure joy began to inch way up to my neck, elevating to over my chin, until it contorted my lower face in a Cheshire Cat's gleeful grin. An unbearably intense 30 seconds later, the tidal surge was replaced by a less extreme but more constant stream of chemical white-hot radiance. My vision returned, and I exhaled with a WHOOSH!!! and picked myself up, my hands-on-knees becoming a hands-in-air while I yowled wildly straight up to the ceiling and joined the rest of the revelers at the smack-dab center of the crowded dancefloor.

The high perfectly cured my afflictions: visions of and longings for Seventh Heaven shot through me as my petulant irritability melted away into energized serenity, and my moroseness and sadness transitioned into delirious bliss. I skipped around the dance floor like a carefree youngster on a children's playground, and regrouped with my now "Dealer-For-Life" in the main arena in front of the DJ booth, bear-hugging and high-fiving him. Sam lifted his hockey-mask off his face and guffawed silently in the ultra-loudness, the lasers making his sweaty pale face glow alien green in the subterranean seascape of that dark patchily lit warehouse, then wagged his finger, vindicated, all smiles now and all good, and yelled, "See, Jay? I told you so!"

And then, as I wandered off to find a space for myself on the dancefloor, I saw a girl in the crowd, someone essentially anonymous—faceless and unidentified—but her nubile body undeniably stood out from the crowd. Clad in curve-hugging white jeans, encased in cutoff T-shirt, with a belly button ring and sporting athletic sneakers, she moved in place with a wild, hurried urgency, as if under great duress. She alternated between wide and narrow stances, poising on one foot and then the other, balancing a bend at the knees, restlessly fluttering her arms, gripping glowsticks in her hands, gyrating her hips, elbowing outwardly one or two at a time, leaning at the chest backwards or forwards, tossing her tied-back hair in a devil-may-care attitude, turning her neck every which way. The music was calling her, compelling her to dance, sort of like how a catchy pop tune makes you want to tap your foot, but in this case her whole body moved in coordinated fashion to the throbbing beat, not just any one isolated appendage. The strobes highlighted and accentuated this amazing spectacle while the green lasers shot through the darkness to put her center stage. And, to anybody who bothered to observe, she was clearly under the influence. That kind of complete and total loss of inhibition in a strange dark place, in the presence of shadowy strangers, the very environment that would make any straightedge partyer duck and run for cover, was unheard of unless some very pure and very strong pills were circulating throughout the party.

So it all came together—the dancing, the clothes, the music, the lights, the drugs—in other words, a pop subculture's own version of Richard Wagner's *gesamtkunstwerk*, or "total art work." Never mind that the dancing was not the highly choreographed expressions of the Bolshoi. Give it a rest that the clothes were not haute couture from Givenchy. Forget that the keyboard chords were not performed on a Steinway. Who cared if the laser lights were not the precision-guided high-frequency medical lasers used to battle cancerous tumors? No matter that the street drug XTC was not under any strict quality control like the psychotropic medication Prozac. And did it register to anyone that the entire experience could be chalked up to nothing more than a raw, savage sensory overload? No. The whole totality of it was downright mysterious and mystical, as if something was going on that I couldn't quite grasp, just at the edge of my comprehension, and yet I knew it felt right. And seeing her was perhaps a "Eureka!" moment, maybe also an epiphany, but I think it was a vision of Beauty with a capital "B" that caught me, totally transfixed and completely riveted, in the whole aesthetic experience. And at that moment, I despaired of ever wanting to see anything else—or anybody else—ever again.

I accosted her, trying desperately to make frantic small talk with this specter, this sprite, amidst all the lasers and lights, awash in the sound and fury.

"Isn't this a great party?!" was my opening line.

"Yeah! What's your name?"

"MY NAME IS JAY!!!"

"Hey, I'm Clarissa! What's up?!"

What's up? I'll show you what's up! I gave her a show of my winning Cheshire Cat's grin, and then the conversation ground to a halt as I grabbed her to me and planted a sloppy wet kiss on her neck, moved up to her cute face, and shoved my tongue deep inside her mouth, while we hopped unabated up and down to the beat. *Holy shit, this stuff really changes your personality!* I had never been that forward with a girl before. If I weren't completely bonkers, I might have stopped to think twice before finding out that her gangster boyfriend was going to kick my ass, or her gangster lesbian girlfriend was going to kick my ass, or her bisexual partners were going to kick my ass, or her transsexual lover was going to kick my ass, for that matter. But I didn't care, I just didn't care. Under the urgent imperatives of the XTC, I grabbed one of her belt loops and started following her around, bouncing to the beat, trailing her like an adolescent bunny rabbit.

She navigated the floor and meandered to her circle of fellow partygoers camped out to the side, with their backpacks and jackets strewn about. While I hopped in place to the beat, she carried on an inaudible conversation with one of her friends. *What are they talking about?* Her friends were ravers of slight build, so at least I wasn't about to get beat up by some seven-foot brother, but I couldn't understand why she wanted to talk at that moment. *Let's either dance, fuck or both, but forget talking!* After about 60 seconds of bouncing around in one place, and her talking to someone whom I couldn't care less about, she turned to me and asked what I was doing after the party. I told her: YOU.

*****

The high lasted from one-thirty to five-thirty, with those hours replete with wild, frenzied bouts of dancing interspersed with random periods of social interaction with others equally as high as I was. God, I must have made a million new friends at that party. I only stopped for water breaks and to smoke a spliff with Sam and his crew, in order to perpetuate and punctuate the high. There were so many pretty girls…the XTC high turned the libido up a notch, although the whole experience was more strongly erotic than merely sexual.

Between five-thirty and seven o'clock, the XTC wore off slowly in an "afterglow," with traces of the initial high tapering off and lingering on. The energy in the warehouse wound down considerably, as less dancing, less partyers, less conversation, and less interesting music registered their presence. People were sitting down or standing up, just talking, not dancing. By seven o'clock, the horizon began to lighten into a blue-grey from dark black, which could be seen through the rows of dirty, dank windows positioned on the upper walls of the warehouse. By eight, Sam was rounding up the troops, and I made sure to navigate back to where everybody in our group had pitched their tents away from the dancefloor. I sure didn't want to get stuck there without a ride back, and I knew I had to be smart about that. Still, there was something that I needed to do right away. I caught up with Clarissa and as I held her hand, I asked her to come home with me. She nodded yes. I led her back to my group.

"Yo, Jay, are you ready to take off?" Sam yelled above the music when he saw me and Clarissa. I pointed to her and asked in confidence to him if there was space in the car for me "plus one." He nodded his assent after scanning to see who I was holding hands with.

"We're ready to go!" I yelled, as she and I stood soaking with sweat through and through, shivering in the uninsulated warehouse into which a chilly New England autumn morning had started to seep in as partygoers began to drift out of the scene. Clarissa and I stood there, holding each other close, keeping our body temperatures up through mutual contact. She trusted me to know where we were going, because although she was a local girl, she'd never been to Harvard.

Our group exited the warehouse as the newly risen sun's rays cast yellow light on our pale faces. We piled into the car, this time a coed group with Clarissa and I huddled in the back seat, Sam in the front passenger seat with Jessica perched on his lap and the designated driver at the helm. It was deafeningly silent as my ears rang with the echoes of phantom bass beats. My whole body trembled from the freezing morning cold that penetrated my sweat-soaked clothes, and the powerful chemical assault that still cast its spell over me. Nobody was doing much talking. When I and Clarissa stepped out of the car back at Harvard Square, ready to retire after the biggest party night of my life, I parted ways with Sam with a simple "Yo, man…we need to hang out more often." Truer word was never spoken, I tell you.

"You got it, dog…we'll do it again," he replied, nodding nonchalantly and smiling good-naturedly, the sunlight brightening his face.

And so that was the start of the party!

*****

While my physical relationships were with rave girls and club-kids, my relations with the women of Harvard were typically Platonic, consisting of friendly affectionate feelings for the opposite sex which were never sexually consummated. I wasn't the only one on campus going to raves and clubs. A pair of Harvard students in particular—Aidan and Amian—entered the scene. Aidan's baggy jeans hid her shapely porcelain-pale legs and her pink hair fell softly past her pale neck and down her back, over the top of her cherry red sweater. Amian's short, boyishly cropped brown hair nicely complimented her olive-colored skin.

One time we packed ourselves up in the station wagon, departed Cambridge at 10 o'clock on a Saturday night and drove to a rave on the farthest tip of Long Island.

"Jay, do you know how to get there?" Aidan checked from the front passenger seat, her attitude all business. She unfolded the map tucked into her side door pocket…ah, the days before GPS.

"Yeah, I have the directions right here. It may take a while," I reassured and cautioned her as I nodded toward the map. I steered the car southward along a darkened highway.

"Wake me up when we get there!" Amian squealed from the back seat, covering herself with a blanket. Her T-shirt and track jacket could barely conceal her protruding breasts.

"Oh, Amian, you're always such a slacker!" Aidan peeved, and I sensed the beginning of a rift between the two friends. "I hope we find good drugs tonight at the party. I feel like XTC." That was probably not smart, in fact. We should have gone with Sam on this one. But he didn't have any XTC at the time.

"Yeah, well, I'd rather do acid, hon," Amian retorted from the back seat. I guess we were taking our chances that night. And I suppose that if sex were in order, I'd have that, too.

Another pair of young ladies also entered the picture around this time. Eliza did women's crew and was from San Francisco's tony Nob Hill, while Liz was a lacrosse-soccer-field hockey triple threat and a third-generation Harvard legacy.

"Hey Jay, what's going on?!" Eliza would chirp excitedly, stopping by Clav-5, looking for a party and enveloping me in a big bear-hug. She was tall and muscular, in contrast to my slight "homeless waif" build.

"Hey Eh-lai-zah, I missed you!" I would flirt, getting up to return her hug and tapping her curvaceous butt playfully. "I missed you, too, Jay!" she flirted back, humping me lightheartedly before I returned to the couch.

But with Liz, the conversation was not so much a contact sport.

"Watcha got there, Liz?" I'd ask her, pointing at the open tome on the desk she was sitting at in her bedroom.

"Oh, just Anna Karenina," Liz would reply, looking drearily bored by the prospect of reading over 800 pages of exposition.

"When do you have to finish that by?" I inquired, remembering that the one time I had picked up Anna Karenina, I had immediately put it down, completely daunted by its sheer length.

"I have to write a paper on it by Monday," Liz mumbled, looking down at the ground.

And here it was, Friday night. Bummer!

"Well, good luck with that and have fun reading it…" I offered with as much contrived enthusiasm as I could muster, while I stared, beady-eyed, at her fine features and toned body.

Eliza and Liz were the cultural opposites of Aidan and Amian. Eliza and Liz belonged to the blonde-haired, blue-eyed WASP establishment, adhered to the all-American scholar-athlete ideal, and were members of the beer and pot crowd. As for Aidan or Amian, they more or less aligned themselves with the colored-haired, dark-eyed counterculture, stayed true to the artsy-fartsy nightclub and rave set, and enjoyed the XTC and acid crowd.

Still, the commonalities were just as pronounced as the differences: they all went to Harvard, they all were smart and they all were beautiful. Being that they were at such close and constant proximity on campus and that our paths crossed frequently, I didn't dare engage too intimately with them, in case a lover's spat broke out. I had learned from a young age, because many of my authority figures were ball-busting females, to think twice before making an enemy of a woman, and the last thing I wanted was a reenactment of a scene from Fatal Attraction or Basic Instinct. And their intelligence was quite off-putting: they weren't like the bimbo rave girls and club chicks whom I had always had wrapped around my finger; now I became afraid of the same thing happening to me. And their beauty meant that most men were at their beck and call. Clearly, beauty and intelligence in a woman were an unbeatable combination. And with nowhere to escape to or hide away on campus, these women were just downright dangerous.

But it wasn't all just about them. I had to turn the lens of examination upon myself: was I a bad boy, just trying to get in their pants, hoping for a quick fling? Or was I a nice guy, looking to get involved with someone whom I genuinely cared about, hoping for a love affair? If I were confused about my own intentions, what possible ideas do you think these women had about my intentions? The potential for misunderstanding, conflict and interpersonal strife was simply too great. Given the romantic minefield in front of me, I began to have a relatively painless, one-sided relationship with drugs. It would be a short-lived tryst, though, for the drugs' seductiveness would take me down a path of no-return, one that would nearly end in my total destruction.

CHAPTER FOUR

THE PHILOSOPHY OF IMMANUEL KANT

While my sideways creep into drugs and raves went on through the Fall of 1994, I was busy in the midst of four classes. But the only one that mattered to me was the tutorial on the German philosopher Immanuel Kant taught by Teaching Fellow Arata.

Seminars, or "tutorials" as they called them at Harvard, were distinguished from classes because tutorials had small attendances and were conducted by Teaching Fellows, whereas classes were taught by professors and were much larger in terms of number of students. For our Kant tutorial, we were in the first floor of Emerson Hall, in a rectangular room with a chalkboard (this was before whiteboards and dry-erase markers) on the near wall and an alcove of windows on the other end, with a conference room table in the center paralleling the rectangular shape of the room. We students sat on the three sides of the table farthest from the chalkboard. Even so, there was nowhere to hide!

I remember Arata arriving for the initial introductions. He stood by the chalkboard and faced us as we sat. His black sweater covered a white collared shirt showing at the neck, with dark jeans and black boots completing the look. He was of medium build and of Asian ethnicity, specifically of Japanese extraction as I concluded from his name. His thick-lensed, horn-rimmed eyeglasses did not flatter his otherwise handsome features, which made me chuckle inwardly. Arata seemed nervous…he shifted from one foot to the other, and he couldn't maintain eye contact with any of us. Rather, he just looked down at the floor. I sensed something amiss, and when he began talking, it became apparent what was bothering him.

"So, my name is, is, Arata, and, uh, I am your, uh, Teaching Fellow, uh, yes, for this…this tutorial."

Oh my God, it's going to be a long semester. It was painful to hear his halting speech. It wasn't outright stuttering, but it did register a severe lack of facility with words. I had already begun to write him off.

"Why, eh, don't we, go, go, around, and, uh, introduce ourselves, um, yes, to each other?"

Strangely enough, while he lacked communication skills, he apparently was a marvelous paper-writer. I once visited him during office hours in the basement of Emerson Hall, and his desk was strewn with papers written by him that were all letter-graded A+ or percentage-graded 100%. I had a discussion about this phenomenon with my professor father, who told me that a lot of graduate students are like that, in the sense that their strengths usually lay either in writing or speaking, but very rarely equally in both. I could relate, but in a different way; it would be as if I were expected to be just as proficient with numbers as with words.

Two fellow classmates, Celeste and Paul, were most demonstrative of the diversity in the room. Celeste was a West Coast transplant from Los Angeles. She was the child of an African-American music mogul and a white TV sitcom starlet. She had had every advantage: grew up in the wealthy neighborhood of Bel-Air, went to the finest schools, wore fashionable name-brand clothes, had an army of coaches and tutors. She was also incredibly attractive; her tan mixed-race skin glowed healthily, showing off to maximum effect her balanced, well-proportioned features, while her designer outfits hugged her petite, curvy body. We had met as freshmen because she and I occasionally hung out with the kids down at the other end of the hall from my suite of rooms in Weld. She was a religion concentrator, not philosophy; for her, this tutorial was an elective. She was, despite her fame, very agreeable and amiable, with none of the neurotic hang-ups that many at Harvard struggled with at the time (myself included). Her situation spoke to Harvard in the 1990s: 30 years after the Civil Rights Movement, you could no longer predict socio-economic status from race. Being African-American no longer meant automatically that you were disadvantaged or poor, any more than being Caucasian automatically meant that you were advantaged and rich.

Now Paul was a different story. Paul was a blonde-haired, blue-eyed fellow who hailed from deepest New England. He, too, had had every advantage: educated at a major private boarding school on the upper East Coast, raised in the exclusively wealthy neighborhoods of Connecticut, wore nothing less than the finest haberdashery, had private teachers and instructors to cater to any and all of his academic needs. If he hadn't been a legacy of sorts, I would have been very surprised. He was rather normal and well-adjusted, a plain man with plain tastes who suffered no physical or mental malady that I could detect, a member of the White Anglo-Saxon Protestant gentry, if I may use the term without its pejorative connotation.

Celeste and Paul were worlds apart, and even though they sat literally inches next to each other at the same conference room table for our weekly discussions, they did not converse openly. There was no communication whatsoever, possibly characteristic of feelings of contempt or scorn each had for the other's background. But they did talk to me, not necessarily because I was from their neck of the woods, nor because I was a V.I.P., but probably because they could tell I was absolutely in love with college. I loved the freedom, I loved the choices, I loved the experimentation, and I loved the alternative lifestyles.

As Celeste and I sat down next to each other in a general common area just outside the classroom during a break in the tutorial, we recounted our previous weekends.

"Hey Jay, how was your weekend? Did you go to a rave?" Celeste asked matter-of-factly.

"Yeah, I did. XTC is such a fun drug; I've never had that much fun in my life," I said, grinning from ear to ear. I don't know why I told her that, but I guess it was because I trusted her, and also because I wanted to impress her with my "cool" drug use. Yeah, right, REAL cool.

"Oh yeah, XTC is a lot of fun, totally," she replied, looking away. I didn't know what she meant. What? Had she done it before? I didn't bother asking; the moment passed.

At least I guess she could tell I was telling the truth, because by this time I was always wearing baggy pants, an apple hat, flat-soled skate shoes and T-shirts in the dead of winter or short-sleeved plaid patterned tops, and no longer skinny blue jeans, leather boots and flannel shirts, as I had as a freshman.

And as for Paul, I recall leaving the seminar one day and walking out the door into the cool November night air with him, his bike in tow.

"So, you really got that idea of the Kantian synthetic a priori down pat, didn't you?" Paul offered as an opening.

"Peshaw, if I can remember what exactly I just said!" I replied good-naturedly, to which we both laughed.

"Well, I tell you, I really struggled with it," Paul admitted.

To that I rejoined, "Well, it's a pretty difficult concept to understand."

"I'm sure you'll figure out the categorical imperative too next week! See you next time!" Paul quipped, as we parted ways and said our goodbyes.

*****

There were three texts for the seminar: *The Critique of Pure Reason, The Critique of Practical Reason* and the *Grounding for the Metaphysics of Morals*.

The Critique of Pure Reason presented itself right away as a challenge. It was really awful stuff, full of horrid circumlocutions, intellectual double-talk, and verbose gobbledygook. It was also quite thick, at hundreds of pages of length. What a total crock of shit. Obviously Kant had a lot of time on his hands to write such a tome. The cover itself was pitch-black and uninspiring, except for an illustration of three colored concentric circles—

pink, light blue, and yellow—which made absolutely no sense. Again, very boring, and even, dare I say, downright ugly. *Don't judge a book by its cover, eh? Yeah, right. I beg to differ*. This was the sort of stuff that, after reading a few paragraphs of stilted gibberish, would leave me either despondent from its difficulty or driven to fury by its impenetrability, or otherwise just aching to take a nap.

However, I bounced back with the *Critique of Practical Reason*, for which I was genuinely interested in the arguments for the Existence of God and the Immortality of the Soul. As no one in my immediate family had ever been of the churchy type, I had thus never encountered anybody I had grown up with, whether family or friends or teachers or colleagues of my father, who ever discussed anything remotely having to do with God or the Soul. At a young age I had concluded that I was agnostic: I hadn't shut the door in God's face just yet, but I was pretty sure that the universe was empty. However, that was a very unreflective, uninformed position. No one had ever discussed whether or not the Soul is immortal in dinner conversation, or in the high school classroom. It just wasn't a topic that I was ever aware of having existed, and even if we had discussed the issue, I would probably have pleaded ignorance. But now, after reading Kant and having the material with which to develop an informed opinion, I sharpened my defense of agnosticism:

First of all, no one truly knows for certain what happens to people after they die. On one hand, the atheists claim that once you are physically dead, then you cease to exist; you are six feet under, pushing up daisies. On the other hand, you have the religious, pious and devout claiming that there is a Soul or Spirit that endures into the afterlife, with God in Heaven waiting for us. This schism alone is good cause for concern. But second of all, modern science still does not have the ability to send people to their death and then return them to life, to tell the rest of us what exactly happened during their sojourn. Thus, we do not have solid evidence or incontrovertible proof as to which side the Truth is on, and there is no way for certain that the debate can be resolved. This, I believe, is a more studied understanding of agnosticism.

The third reading, the *Grounding for the Metaphysics of Morals*, made my appreciation for Kant's worldly observations most permanent and lasting. Even today, I have a copy of the work in my small book collection. Kant exhorts his readers to gain the ability to be understood (i.e., generally intelligible) without, in the same breath, losing the ability to provide knowledge (i.e., basic insight). I was overjoyed by the first section's first paragraph of James W. Ellington's 1993 interpretation for Hackett Classics: "There is nothing in the world, or even out of it, that can be called good without qualification, except a good will…" So here is a thinker who believes that having moral intentions is more valuable than possessing the things most people typically regard as unconditionally good, such as money, fame, or health! What struck me was Kant's fine prose style, but not in an academic, stuffy way, mind you. He wrote intelligently without arid formalism, with importance but without bombast. Although the text was originally German, the excellence of Ellington's English translation stood out in bringing the true sense of the original to the English reader. The particular turns of phrase and uses of idiomatic expressions made the prose lucid despite the abstract heavy-handedness of the subject matter. This was writing I had never experienced reading before, quite unlike the back-and-forth verbal sparring of the Socratic dialogues, longer and more engaged in argument than the textual fragments of the pre-Socratics, and deeper and more profound than the Hellenistic schools of philosophy.

I had to write a term paper, which I entitled "Immanuel Kant and His Dream of the Highest Good," and it was based on a passage from *The Critique of Practical Reason*. I decided to work on it late at night, about 12 hours before it was due, as that was my habit during sophomore year, to just cram things at the last minute. The old habits of high school had not been as formally ingrained as everyone had thought; the emotional impulsiveness that I indulged and which incentivized my alcohol and pot habits pre-college was still there. The funny thing was that I was still under the influence of the XTC I had taken on Saturday night, and here it was on

Sunday night, in "Clav-5," with the biting frost of a chilly Boston fall evening descending upon the windows of our warm, lamp-lit room. But I had to discipline my mind and churn out this paper…

Kant's vision of a Highest Good is commensurate with his membership in the tradition of German transcendental idealism. Kant attempts to achieve this dream of his with...

And on and on and on. During the writing of the term paper, I had to balance both the intellectual high obtained from reading Kant with the blissful feelings that I was still experiencing from just the other night. I thought that I could handle it in a cinch: exerting my brain powerfully in novel and sophisticated ways while handicapping that same organ's highest and most complex faculties. This was an entirely new experience for me: could I enjoy a drugged high and an intellectual high at the same time? In high school, I hadn't tried to party and study at the same time. That would have been like sitting down to a marijuana spliff while reading Julius Caesar: it simply wouldn't have worked. On weekdays, I was with the valedictorian cohort in class, and on weekends, I was with the cool kids at the party. I had neither been impaired in the classroom, nor sober at the party, for that matter. Even as a Harvard freshman, I was never inebriated in the lecture hall. But this delightful and dangerous exercise was pushing the envelope in ways that I couldn't have possibly fathomed. I was basically being bit by the philosophy bug and getting stung by a drug habit at the same time: Kant was a hard thinker, and XTC was a hard drug. Depending on whom you asked, I was either getting pulled in opposite directions or creating quadruple synergies.

Looking back on that time, I can't for a second believe that I could have written anything remotely coherent while my mind was so heavily intoxicated. Still, I have noticed that some people seem to function better when under the influence. I certainly saw that in Sam, who became more and more sober the more drugs he ingested; apparently it didn't matter that he got high on his own supply. But I wasn't like him. I couldn't hide my addiction from anybody, least of all from myself. True, I got an A- on the paper from Arata, and a B+ for the semester. But I also heard from the grapevine that he was a relatively easy grader, so it was just a tilt towards deception.

*****

At this time, my roommates were also starting to delve into their respective concentrations. Smurfy's was American history, Kee's was English, and Jerseyboy's was pre-med. Smurfy and Kee were the ones I could best hold an intellectual conversation with, given that history and English both belonged with philosophy as humanities concentrations. Jerseyboy could hold his own in a college bull session; he had a very strong common sense about him that he wielded effectively in conversation. But his orientation to the world was still different from that of us other three.

"So I learned of Immanuel Kant's categorical imperative today," I grinned, excited about what I had learned, and joining the three of them relaxing one day in the alcove located in a corner of Clav-5.

"Wait, wait, wait, isn't that the Golden Rule, do unto others as you would have them do unto you?" Kee pushed back intellectually. He had heard of the Golden Rule in English literature, and was trying to make a connection.

Backpedaling, I began slowly, "Well, it's similar but there's an important distinction. The Golden Rule expresses how you would treat others as it is acceptable to your standards, whereas Kant's categorical imperative expresses how you would treat others as it is acceptable to their standards," I rebounded.

"So WHEN and WHERE was Kant's categorical imperative discovered?" Smurfy inquired, shooting me full of word-bullets. He was trying to locate the concept from a historical perspective in order to place it alongside other intellectual developments and events of that time, specifically in the United States.

"In the late 1700s in Konigsberg," I responded to Smurfy, put off by his interrogation.

"Jay, are you reading this stuff in German or in English?" Jerseyboy interjected as he cut into the stream of conversation. Jerseyboy knew how to cut to the bone with matter-of-fact and relevant questions, even though he was not necessarily connected to the liberal arts tradition.

"Err, in English translation," I replied sheepishly, as I began to feel that maybe I should be reading Kant in the original German, since reading him in English might be a poor substitute for the real thing.

"Oh, OK," Jerseyboy mumbled as he ended his line of questioning there.

"Any other questions, gentlemen?" I finished rhetorically, feeling verbally abused. Sometimes they could really get on my nerves. I sat down to have a hit of marijuana from our red plastic water bong, otherwise known as the Red Monster. In jest, we had affixed on the tube portion of the bong a sticky label listing emergency contact numbers for police, fire and ambulance services. As with the term paper and XTC afterglow, the categorical imperative and weed-smoking would go hand in hand. I would spend so much mental effort learning these philosophical concepts and principles, and then just like that, poof! All of it would literally go up in smoke. What a waste…

*****

One morning in my sophomore fall semester, as I was playing Miles Davis's "Kind of Blue" on my regular two-hour weekly radio program, one of the studio phone lines started blinking. I had no idea who it was, so I gave the old jingle, "Harvard Radio, this is Jay speaking, how can I help you?"

"Jay, it's Nathan!" Nathan was a junior-year Jazz DJ. I had come to know him as a bossy type of guy, a real Mister Know-It-All.

"Hi Nathan! What's up? What's going on?"

"Jay, listen to me! You play the same old shit all the fucking time. You play 'Kind of Blue' week in and week out! This is like Jazz's Greatest Hits! Everybody plays this stuff! C'mon, learn to STRETCH yourself and broadcast more interesting and better jazz, OK?!"

"Yeah Nate, thanks for the suggestion," I retorted dismissively, hanging up on him as I bit my tongue, gritted my teeth and cursed him under my breath. It's true, I played "Kind of Blue" every week, but it was good music, plus it calmed my sadness. Jolted by the harsh criticism, I muttered to myself, *Nathan, you pompous asshole!* I returned to the stacks, this time taking an alternate route, still stung by the criticism…

*****

One afternoon in my sophomore spring semester, I was checking my mail when there was this standard-size envelope lying flat in my cubbyhole. Not bothering to inspect the outside, I cut it open, from which out slipped two things: a small ivory-colored card of heavy stock, folded on a crease with fine print on the inside, and a size-matched stamped return envelope addressed to Murr Center, 65 North Harvard Street, Boston, MA 02163.

What is this? Curious, I read the fine print: an invitation to be an honorary member of the Harvard Varsity Club. Mystified, I reached back into memory: I had played lacrosse, but that was freshman lacrosse, not junior varsity, let alone varsity, and I hadn't played any other sport. Baffled, I thought about the situation for a minute. Other people were checking their mail, so I stepped to the side, mulling it over. *Must be a clerical error...if I send it in and cause administrative confusion, someone might get in trouble*. Certain that I was doing somebody a favor, I carefully returned the contents back into the outer envelope, ripped it up a couple times for good measure, and threw it in the trash. Out of sight, out of mind. I paid it no heed after that.

CHAPTER FIVE

WHAT A LONG STRANGE TRIP IT'S BEEN

Grade-wise, sophomore year was a step down from year previous: 3 B+'s and 4 B's. After my sophomore year, when I returned to Pittsburgh in August 1995 to spend some time that summer with my parents, I asked Dad to let me take a year off. We sat down at opposite ends of the dinner table, I in my baggy pants and oversize T-shirt, Dad in blue oxford dress shirt and khakis.

"Dad, I'd like to take a year off from Harvard."

"OK, so what're you going to do for a year?"

"I don't know, maybe I'll work," I said, somewhat listlessly.

"No, Jay, this won't do. You just can't come back here, OK? If you have a plan that would be one thing, but right now you have nothing but a vague idea of what you want to do instead. So you will finish up at Harvard."

"Yes, Dad."

Glumly I boarded the plane back to Cambridge for junior year, with a downturned pout on my face for the whole flight after the father-son conversation, an expression reflecting separate but equal parts deflation and upset. During the whole plane ride, part of me felt like collapsing in my seat, weighted under by the burden of parental expectations and societal obligations. Yet at the same time, I wanted to jump out of the same seat, to do battle with imaginary would-be captors in righteous indignation of Fate. I was pulled in opposite directions, and the internal conflict felt completely awkward and totally uncomfortable.

But in reality, my father knew better. If I had relinquished the initiative at the midway point of college, chances are I wouldn't have finished. The time to take time off was after high school and before the start of college, so as to take a breather to adjust. But leaving in the middle of it all would have been inadvisable. So just as much as I was upset by the decision, it was ultimately to stand me in good stead.

*****

But as I began junior year, I tossed off all passing restraint when I reunited in Clav-5 with my roommates for another round of school. It was warm and sunny in the waning days of summer break, but a nip of autumn was in the air just before the start of classes. My giddy upbeat mood, triggered by the freedom I felt on campus, 571.2 miles away from the stern visage of my father and the anxious gaze of my mother, infected my roommates for them to also ditch restraint and party on. Hell, my own moods infected even me! Kee and I conferred to make plans for an acid trip, giggling like little school children in anticipation. First stop: Sam's den for a drug deal.

I picked up the phone off the handset (cordless just coming into vogue back then), and called Sam up.

"Hey Sam, how's it going?" I mustered charm in my voice.

"What's up, Jay?" If a voice could have facial expressions, this one of Sam's would be expressionless.

"I need your help. I need your help bigtime!" I giggled nervously.

"Oh, yeah? Help on what?" Again, if a voice could have facial expressions, this one of Sam's would be barren.

"You know!" I laughed uncontrollably.

"No, I don't know…" Now I was sure I could detect an amused half-smile.

"Dude, I need some FUCKING DRUGS, man!" I expressed with moral outrage.

"Jesus Christ, Jay, don't say that! Get your ass over here…I'll see you in a little bit." He started giggling now, exasperated at my circumlocutions.

"See you soon!" Click.

I hotfooted it over there. A little social greasing of the wheels was in order initially. *Hey, Sam, how are you? Good to see you! Say, did you hear about that party going down this coming weekend?* Then, down to business.

"Whassup dawg, I need two hits of acid. For me and Kee."

"OK, I just got in some Circles."

"Sure, how much? Just two."

"Twenty bucks."

Sam pulled out a suitcase from under his bed, flipped out the top half, and began riffling through the belongings with the familiarity of an intimate owner. From an all-purpose trusty sandwich bag, he pulled out a blotter sheet with a pattern of roundish objects on one side which identified the acid as such.

He undid two hits for me. In exchange, I placed an Andrew Jackson into his open hand. By the time his hand closed down on the twenty, the enormity of what we had done, something illegal and unlawful, a criminal act, as it were, made us closer than romantic lovers, more intimate than battlefield comrades, as if we were joined at the hip. If he got caught for distribution, I would go down for possession. And if I got caught for possession, he would go down for distribution.

Now I had to ungrease the wheels this time: *Hey, Sam, why don't you come over and smoke some pot with us in Claverly 5? We should do dinner at Adams House sometime; I'll get you in past the cashier, OK? Alright, see you next time!*

And out the door…

*****

Getting back hurriedly to Claverly, grinning mischievously as the Friday sun set, I confirmed the sale with Kee, who peered closely through the plastic sandwich bag wrap at the acid tabs before putting both in the bag into his pocket. I guess he thought I was his errand boy. But what did it matter to me? I just wanted to party. We planned to take them after dinner that early evening, and it was six o'clock already.

Kee and I scurried over to the cafeteria and grabbed a plate of all-purpose spaghetti with meat sauce, along with a ubiquitous soda and juice mixture. We just wanted anything with protein, carbs and fluid that would get us through the long night. And boy, what a night it would be, although in ways I would never have imagined!

After scarfing down our dinner portions, we rushed back to the confines of our room. In high spirits, I sat down on the edge of my bed as Kee administered last rites. "Down the hatch!" Kee hee-heed as he tore the blotter in two and placed one of the two pieces on my tongue. It had no taste, but my saliva quickly processed the paper and then I swallowed the remaining wet wad. I wasn't paying any attention to Kee at that moment, but when I looked up he was giggling hysterically with a crazed glint in his eye and an evil grin on his mouth, all in anticipation.

Time for a victory cigarette; Kee and I lit up, the glowing ends making random patterns in the air, as the stereo blared out the thumping four-to-the-floor of a familiar house music beat mixed by DJ Doc Martin. We started dancing in the middle of the room, our flat-soled sneakers bouncing up and down on the brown-gray rug, our light fall windbreakers billowing outward, baggy jeans creasing where they loosely folded, baseball caps shielding our faces from direct view. Nothing was happening yet, but we knew something would; Sam wouldn't let us down!

Kee took over the direction of the two-man party. "Let's take a walk, Jay!"

"Whatever you say, man!" I acquiesced in an amiable and good-natured tone.

Already bundled up for the autumn breezes, we treaded lightly down the stairs and out the front entrance of Claverly Hall, stepping down to start our journey on the red-brick cobblestone sidewalk. There was palpable excitement in the air for us as we headed up the sloping Plympton Street, which went past the thick iron-wrought gates of Adams House and toward Harvard Yard's maze of concrete walkways. Passing through Harvard Yard brought up memories of freshman year in Weld Hall. Finally we pushed onward to Memorial Hall, a giant lecture hall where the Economics 10 lectures of Professor Martin, President Ronald Reagan's economic adviser, were held. Ah, did I hate those stupid lectures of sophomore year! So dry, boring and uninteresting!

"Hey Kee, remember that philosophy class we took together freshman year?"

"Yeah, the professor…she had a shaved head, like a drill sergeant."

"Hee-hee, sure, I know…"

The inside jokes crackled between Kee and me as we passed these landmarks. Ah boy, the waning days of summer and the coming nights of autumn…

Then something changed in my emotional attitude as we passed Memorial Hall and continued on the red brick road alongside the Science Center. The joy was flipped right over and immediately into an impending sense of doom. My anticipation of the acid high morphed into agitation, now that I was in it. The joking and laughter died and became anxiety and barely restrained terror. This was turning into a bad trip!

I turned to Kee and advised, "You know what? We should get back to the room." I was starting to worry.

"Oh God, yeah, I think you're right." Concern colored his voice, too.

We made an about-face, and I have no idea how we made it back in that worsening condition, with the acid slowly but surely taking over our minds.

*****

The next thing I remember was Kee and I sitting in the common area of our room, caught up in an increasingly incoherent conversation. He was starting to deteriorate mentally, and it was all I could do to put up the bravest stonewall against a shitty acid trip with his outrageous behavior heaped on top.

"Oh Jay! My parents have no idea what Harvard is like!" He took out his wallet and opened it up to drop all his money bills and ID cards inside onto the floor. "You see that, Jay? You see that? That's Harvard! That's Harvard, Jay! It doesn't matter! All of this DOESN'T FUCKING MATTER!"

I sat in silence opposite Kee on the couch, holding my broken head in my hands.

"Kee, take it EASY, man…"

"Come on, Jay," Kee shouted, as he took off his pants, revealing his hospital-white, loose-fitting boxers. "LET'S SHOW 'EM!" he roared and then ran out of the room.

I heard the wooden door slowly close behind him, in contrast to his quick exit, leaving a curious silence after all his hubbub.

That's when, in the midst of the reprieve from the pressure Kee had placed on my really shitty trip, I heard him screaming and raving at the top of his lungs: "I'M A GENIUS! I'M A GENIUS!! I'M A GENIUS!!!" He was basically almost exactly downstairs from where I was, except outside, as I could tell from the ringing of his voice revealing that he was probably sitting on the steps of the front entrance of Claverly Hall, carrying on to anybody and everybody about how much of a crazed lunatic he was.

My vantage point changed, from upstairs looking down over the railing of Clav-5's balcony, to having crept downward on my own fucked-up cognizance to the front entrance of the same building just outside. The traffic that circulated in front of the Harvard Lampoon building and the adjacent Lowell House had stopped, and Kee was in his boxers, facing off, his one versus the many, standing against the traffic, with a dark haunted glare and menacing snarl, while the traffic had momentarily ground to a complete halt. People were getting out of their cars and pointing and laughing at the sorry sight that Kee had become. It was utterly and completely unnerving.

"Jay!" I thought I heard Kee scream.

Oh God, what now? I don't need to be recognized. I turned around.

"Oh Jose!" The security guard had stepped up beside me. I was so relieved to see him, as I felt the pressure that had built up inside of me taper off right away. "Thank God, it's you!"

"Hey, isn't that your boy out there? What's he doing, man?"

"Jose, look man, please…please…just get him off the street…just get him off the street," I pleaded, my mind jackknifing in all directions from the way-too-strong acid.

Alarmed and concerned, Jose replied, "OK bro, I'll see what I can do."

I remember that law enforcement had reached the scene right at that moment, and I saw Jose in his brown outfit surrounded by a sea of blue uniforms, a surreal supergrin on his face, and I knew at that moment, Jose was trying his complete Sunday best to convince the cops that Kee needed to come with him, and not with them. Feeling paranoid and running for cover, I turned back, swiped my keycard to the entrance of Claverly Hall, and ran up the steps to Room 5.

*****

I crept to the balcony window of Clav-5 to look down at a worsening scene. Jose was nowhere in sight. But there was Kee, bent over the hood of a police squad car, with a good half-dozen police officers hovering over him, trying to restrain him. I could see from the occasional convulsions of Kee's body that he was trying with a madman's energy to unloose himself from their grip. It was all they could do to keep him from hurting himself or them.

Then the ambulance screeched to a halt, and in a matter of minutes, Kee was lying partially upright in a stretcher, held in place by cords, and in Kee's upright posture, the most bizarre, ghastliest grin appeared on his face as he shrieked incoherently with laughter. The paramedics loaded him through the back of the ambulance, and that's when the whole scene began to die down.

The paramedics curved away from the scene and up the hill around the corner, heard but not seen, until the ambulance siren could not be heard anymore. The cops returned to their congregated squad cars and peeled away, leaving a deserted street that began to fill with once-again normally flowing traffic.

I lay on that ugly gray-brown carpet, huddled in a fetal position, trying to make sense of the horrifying scene that had just passed, now in a slow transition from RED ALERT back to Situation-Normal-All-Fucked-Up. I stared at Kee's dollar bills, jeans and jacket, lying on the carpet as if tossed there carelessly by someone who had too much money and too many possessions. I remember the door opening behind me and in walking Smurfy with Yori, a fellow Weld fifth floor inmate from freshman year whose rooming group lived directly underneath us in Clav-2.

"Hahahahahhahahahaha, what's going on, guys?" I blabbered off in a shriek.

"Uh, yeah Jay, what's up?" Smurfy asked me, surprised by and suspicious of my hyena-like outburst.

"It's Kee, man, hee hee," I uttered, hysterically giggling against my will. "His clothes, man, his clothes!"

"His clothes, Jay?" Smurfy asked, pointing to the crumpled masses. "What about his clothes?"

"He left them here! He left them with his money and ID!"

"Yeah, well, he'll come back for those, I'm sure. He's probably just doing the laundry."

"No, I'm saying he got taken away. In an ambulance! Ha ha ha ha!"

"What? Jay, that's not funny," Yori said. Smurfy and Yori looked at each other.

"What happened?" Smurfy demanded to know. "What ambulance?"

"Wait, I'm still fucked up! OK, he, uh, hee hee, uh, ha ha, got fucked up and then they took him away!"

Amidst all this confusion, the reality finally emerged an hour later, after I had come down from the acid high, that Kee had been taken away in a stretcher for a bad acid trip. The enormity of the situation was starting to sink in. All I could think of was, *that could have been me.*

The night ended with all of us going to sleep fitfully, knowing that repercussions were in store. The question was, who would be indicted? Just Kee? Or maybe me? Or maybe Sam? How much did the administration know, or would figure out, about what had transpired? How far would they go to punish and prosecute?

*****

The next day, Kee popped up on the scene, clearly in charge of his faculties again. However, I was afraid of him and disturbed to see him there, moving, breathing, talking and deliberating, as if none of the goings-on the night before had happened, as if he had entirely forgotten how horrifying his behavior had been.

"Jay, God damn it, what did I do!? Just tell me, what happened!? What did I fucking do!?" He apparently had no memory of what had occurred.

"I don't know," was all I could muster. I was traumatized, and still couldn't get over the enormity of what had transpired the night before. I had heard they had pumped his stomach at the hospital.

The conversation inside of me completely died whenever he and I were in the same room from that day forward. I just couldn't reconcile the Kee that had been revealed previously with the Kee I was seeing now. It was very disturbing to have him sit next to me as if we were still all "buddy-buddy" after what I had witnessed, after I had just borne witness to that completely bonkers psychotic side of him. I still couldn't figure it out: we had both taken the same number of hits of acid, of the same type, and yet he loses his mind and I didn't…something doesn't add up here. What was going on with him? And why did I emerge relatively unscathed?

The administrative board, or so-called "Ad-Board," which adjudicated on undergraduate disciplinary matters, moved rather procedurally on this one. Kee would be expelled for one year, at which point he could return to his degree program, if he so desired. He was gone shortly after that, with no send-off or anything. Just a simple "pack your bags and go home." An eerie silence now descended over the vacuum of his bedroom. Although he would return, we were stunned by how quickly he had been sent packing by the powers that were. Swift and disproportionate retribution was the name of the Ad-Board's game. The rest of us counted our lucky stars that no one else had been implicated.

*****

Things died down pretty quickly, albeit temporarily, in Clav-5 after that incident. There was the initial shock among all of the people that knew and were friends with Kee. Moreover, we still weren't sure if anybody else had been fingered. But after the dust settled and things returned to a debilitated normalcy, the pot-smoking continued even more so and the drug-doing became even more prevalent.

"Here, hit that, man," Smurfy choked out, as he passed the water bong to me. He was starting to really get on my nerves. Smurfy was the kind of pot-smoker who was *always* down to smoke *your* weed. Everybody paid for their fair share; why couldn't he?

"Today was so fuckin' ill," I complained in street-slang, as I rubbed my face with my hands.

"Just relax and take it easy," Jerseyboy offered nonchalantly while he stuck to his beer and stayed away from the pot.

After Kee's meltdown, I would also head over to Sam's place on a different part of campus and leave my roommates behind at Clav-5 in order to lose myself in the harder drugs.

On one of these visits, Sam offered advice from a different, more American perspective regarding parents: "Jay, I stopped doing things to please my parents a long, long time ago. Just let it go and do what makes you happy!" which I guess for him meant my doing more drugs and hence offering up a bigger profit margin for him. Sensing an ulterior motive in his seemingly altruistic message, I didn't say anything and just nodded in agreement.

For months on end, I just kept sniffing up powders indiscriminately—cocaine, crystal meth, angel dust, ketamine, crack even, and XTC if Sam had it—which gave me temporary relief from stress. But as soon as the high wore off, I was back to square one emotionally, maybe even worse off than I was before. There was no relief in sight. It was a vicious cycle I was now caught up in: partying to excess cognitively impaired me and increased the academic stress I experienced, but the academic stress then gave me an overwhelming excuse to jump back into excessive partying to stop reminding myself of my academic responsibilities.

Relationship-wise, I started substituting drugs for sex. I couldn't bother with the clash of wills, the arguments and fights, the seducing and playing around. Relationships had lost all their fun. Meanwhile, Sam had started *trading* drugs for sex. He would go on with feigned humility and in lurid detail about the next notch in his belt, about this girl or that girl, how he had used her for his own purposes, as if it were all a comical farce. My roommates and I would listen, half-amused, half-disgusted, not sure how to react. Sam liked to play the power game, and he knew drugs were a powerful weapon in his arsenal to induce submission in girls. He really was a modern-day Falstaff, hedonistic and pleasure-seeking, lecherous and sensual. And yes, his influence was strong. But I would break with him just as Prince Hal had done in *Henry IV*. There would be a day of reckoning, when the two of us would part ways.

CHAPTER SIX

GOD IS DEAD

From junior year, doing drugs stopped being an enjoyable pastime, and became a grudging routine full of harmful consequences. No longer a habit pursued for fun, drugs became an addiction pursued out of necessity.

The effects were immediately apparent in my junior-year tutorial on the 19th-century German philosopher Friedrich Nietzsche, a tutorial that I really enjoyed but which was conducted at a time in my college life when I was poorly equipped intellectually and markedly deteriorated emotionally.

I remember that day in September when I first met my cohort. The six of us, including the Teaching Fellow

David, were all men, but I was the only minority. Everybody else was Caucasian. My head was shaved in a mean, punk-like look; everybody else had a full head of hair. I was wearing T-shirts and super baggy pants; everybody else was wearing collared shirts and slim jeans or khakis.

David was a portly gentleman who enjoyed wearing sweaters over dress shirts, with corduroy pants and brown nondescript shoes to finish the look. His curly brown hair and cowlick covered the top of a visage that was in a perpetually wry smile, as if he were reflecting on a bittersweet memory. His eyeglasses offered him a distinguished gaze, but not in a nerdy or four-eyed way.

He started us off in the small conference room. "Hello everyone and welcome. My name is David and I will be your Teaching Fellow for this tutorial on Friedrich Nietzsche's moral philosophy. I trust you have all purchased the volumes listed on the syllabus, and that you will come prepared to work and participate actively in class discussion…"

David struck me as a remarkably educated human being, and to this day I consider him to be my best educator at Harvard. He was also remarkably kind. He took the time to listen to all of us, even me, despite my dubious fashions and halting speech. He never became cross or impatient; he was always tolerant and understanding. He certainly had the most amazing command of the English language that I could remember anybody ever having. Today he is a professor of philosophy in his own right, but even back then at Harvard, as a graduate student he struck me as already deserving to belong on the faculty of a distinguished Department of Philosophy at a prestigious university. His verbal command of the language was quite unlike Arata's, and his comments on my papers were deeper, more insightful and more meaningful than Arata's.

The readings were also remarkable like Kant's were for Arata's sophomore year tutorial, but in a very different way. The list of assigned readings was nothing unusual or out of the ordinary, compared to that of any other undergraduate Nietzsche seminar at an excellent philosophy department: *On the Genealogy of Morals, Ecce Homo, The Antichrist, Beyond Good and Evil.* But the style in which Nietzsche wrote was very different from Kant's. Nietzsche writes aphoristically at times, while Kant could go on garrulously in 50-word sentences. Nietzsche would proceed to assassinate the character of other philosophers (including Kant), whereas Kant generally refrained from personal attacks. When Nietzsche writes at extended length, he does so in a very symbolic and metaphorical way that seduces the reader, whereas Kant could occasionally be accused of being an arid formalist. But whereas I took an immediate liking to Kant's writing without Arata's guidance, David facilitated greatly my developing taste for Nietzsche.

Unfortunately the papers I wrote for his tutorial were shamefully inadequate. David actually had to correct me to use gender-neutral plural terms such as "they" and "them" instead of gender-specific singular terms such as "he/she" or "his/her," obviously very basic rules for writing in non-sexist language. David also had to remind me that the key to reading Nietzsche is not to take him literally, but figuratively, as when Nietzsche writes, "God is dead," he is not really saying that there is no God, but rather that religion in modern times has lost its ability to instill strong beliefs in its adherents. It was completely embarrassing to commit such remedial errors in writing and interpretation. But David took pity on me, and though he should have given me a C or D, he slapped me on the wrist with a B+. I think he remembered that I was very grateful for everything I learned in the tutorial, that my appreciation for Nietzsche made up, if somewhat marginally, for my lack of comprehension of Nietzsche, and that I always showed respect to David without a hint of scorn or contempt, even when, for example, he revealed his personal battle with depression, which I certainly couldn't help but empathize with.

*****

I remember sitting in the tutorial, still coming off the most recent high, on whatever powder that had been offered to me at that time by Sam. I was a mess. I could sit still and listen, but that was because I was in a dumb stupor, not because I was enthralled by the conversation. There was no way I could intelligently process the information coming into my brain; my cognitive development had become impaired. I was operating at a very low level of intellectual sophistication. All I could focus on were the individual words David was so expertly utilizing, and not, more importantly, the general ideas he was trying to convey.

All of us in class were picked out by David to do a class project due in two weeks: to read a section of a Nietzschean text and interpret it within the context of the current in-class discussion. I was given *Ecce Homo's* section on the slave morality called "ressentiment" by Nietzsche. I outwardly complied, but in two weeks, I had no idea what I was dealing with. I arrived two weeks later, and everybody else was well-prepared for their particular readings, some even having 3-ring binders to hand their supplements in with. I didn't have anything printed out, my motivations over the last two weeks bouncing between getting high and getting higher. When it became my turn to discuss my assignment, I stated, with all the certainty of doubt, that "I think there is something wrong with the translation." I didn't have anything even remotely prepared, no reading, no interpretation, no paper, nothing.

To which, David inquired very patiently, looking down humbly, "And what exactly about the translation do you have a problem with?" Again: so benevolent, so kind. And again, I was held speechless by his tolerance of me. He really did take pity on me.

For our final meeting, we sat outside on the grass in the lawn adjacent to Emerson Hall, in the warm spring sun of a bright-lit New England day in April 1996. David was going on with his sophisticated locutions, and at one point I sat there exclaiming, "Oh, that's a good word!" and wrote it down in my notebook for future reference. I'm sure nobody there, neither my classmates nor David, considered me a serious student, one worthy of any consideration for distinction or merit. I received a B for the tutorial, but I knew again that David had slapped me on the wrist, like so many other educators I had encountered before. He should have given me a C, maybe even a D.

The challenge seemed insurmountable: I had a habit that I didn't know how to quit, so I had dug for myself a pretty deep hole. Furthermore, even if I did get out of the hole, how would I elevate to the intellectual heights that my classmates had reached? Things had come to a critical point, where I had crossed the line from problem user to drug addict: the first is drug-dependent and can keep it together, while the second is drug-abusing and can't keep it together. I was an addict, for sure, and it was at that point, during the summer between junior and senior years, that I came to that big realization, that I indeed had a problem. I couldn't hide it anymore. It was out in the open.

*****

Towards the end of the spring semester of 1996, I continued my duties of manning a 2-hour weekly program on WHRB-FM, Harvard Radio. I managed but was reeling from the previous weekend's effects of pot, XTC and other hard drugs. Emotionally, I was weak, vulnerable and defenseless, and whenever I came down off the XTC high and after the afterglow, I could be easily exploited and easily manipulated. I was an emotional trainwreck. Indeed, in the radio station's studio, I became suddenly afraid that my musical selections were not up to par, that somebody in metropolitan Boston would raise hell or that I would draw the ire of yet another Nathan, as had happened before in the sophomore year.

"Welcome to WHRB-FM, 95.3 Harvard Radio… uh, I'm just going to play some music… and please let me know if you like it," I pleaded into the microphone before going off mike and into program. Immediately the phones started ringing.

"Hello, WHRB-FM, how can I help you?"

"Are you the DJ?" It was a man's voice.

"Yes, sir."

"OK, now look, young man, you don't have to ask if we like it or not! This is your radio program and you should play whatever you want to, OK? There's no need for you to ask us if we like it."

Shuddering at the benevolent outburst, all I could muster was "OK, sir, thank you for your comments."

The second phone rang. I picked it up fearfully.

"WHRB-FM, how can I help you?"

"Are you the DJ?" This time it was a woman's voice.

"Yes, I am. How can I help you, Miss?"

"Well, I like the music you're playing. OK?"

Embarrassed that my previous display of weakness required moral support from strangers, and unabashedly grateful for her kind remark, I replied, "Thanks a bunch," and hung up the phone while I rubbed my face in my hands and prayed that God would relieve me of my affliction.

After coming back from that emotionally treacherous radio program, I stopped by the mailboxes to see if I had received anything. There was a standard-size envelope lying flat in my cubbyhole. There was something familiar about the return address: Murr Center. I cut the envelope open, from which slipped out a small card folded once in the middle crease, continuing with a cryptic message on the inside, and a size-matched stamped return envelope for the Harvard Varsity Club.

Wait, a second invitation to join the Club in as many years? I kept thinking to myself: *Why would they keep sending me this? I don't play lacrosse anymore*. I shredded the contents to pieces in my hands, tossed the shreds in the garbage, and stormed out of the mailroom.

CHAPTER SEVEN

WITH HONORS

Back in Pittsburgh during the summer of 1996, after junior year in Cambridge, I knew that my parents wouldn't be happy with my "report card": 1 A-, 2 B+s, 4 Bs and 2 B-s. It was a slip from sophomore year, which in turn was a step down from freshman year. I was going the wrong way. Not much of a decline, of course, just from a B+ average to a B average, but my parents, and especially I myself, wanted to see all A's at Harvard, given that I was giving it my all, 110%. But it was complete ego-destruction, what with me having been the only valedictorian in high school, but now surrounded by valedictorians in the entire Harvard class. I was doing the best I could, given the academic stress and drug problem I was doubly saddled with, and it wasn't enough.

So I started getting angry at myself: I began to turn inward, upon myself, with the voices of the critical individuals surrounding me on campus. When I returned to Boston a few days before the senior semester was about to begin, I locked myself in the summer apartment bathroom one hot and humid afternoon. I looked at myself in the mirror, and asked my reflection a related series of difficult questions: *When am I going to start taking myself seriously? Why am I worse off now than I was before? How am I going to face myself tomorrow if I do nothing about it today?* With these questions, I confronted a moral dilemma. Would I unreflectively "jump through the hoops," and merely "go through the motions," while I relied on and leaned upon classmates' generosity and teachers' largesse to get me through, as I had done these first three years? Or would I take it upon myself to go all out to achieve excellence, and learn to stand on my own two feet, in order to become a civilized, respectable and educated human being, and essentially a true Harvard Man?

I realized as I gazed at myself in the mirror that I had gotten by on a lot of people's good graces; those surrounding me had pretty much always given me the benefit of the doubt, whether my Teaching Fellows, my parents, my roommates or my girlfriends. When would I repay the favor? Instead of sucking everyone else's emotional and mental energies like a galactic black hole, when would I give back to the ones who believed in me and who had been loyal to me?

I came upon a deep epiphany as the remaining days of summer break came to an end. I started to achieve more self-reflective insights into my own condition than before, especially as I was now approaching the "home stretch" of my time at Harvard. I didn't party as much that junior summer, and I kept my distance from my drug-dealer Sam, only occasionally meeting up with him at the local club. College doesn't last forever, and it had never ever occurred to me to graduate on the so-called "five-year plan." It was exhausting to even think about pulling out all the stops for a sprint finish to the end line. Yet I kept wondering how I could achieve that type of finish, and what project would give me the structure to motivate me strongly.

It was almost by accident that I was talking to some fellow classmates about the topic of Hollywood movies with a Harvard theme. There was one in particular that struck me: With Honors, starring Brendan Fraser, about a Harvard student who loses his honors thesis in a Harvard Square storm drain, only to have it repossessed by a bum who returns it to him piece by piece. The title of the movie stayed with me: "With honors," the Latin equivalent being *cum laude*. Hey, I liked that! Jay Hawk Kim, Harvard 1997, *Cum Laude*. Yeah, that had a certain aura of distinction to it, a halo of prestige, if you will.

So I took a trip up to the administrative office of the Philosophy Department on the third floor of Emerson Hall, and talked to Nanette, Harvard Philosophy's Administrative Head. The administration office was nearly always a whirlwind of activity. The dust never settled in that room, what with administrators, professors, grad students and undergrads perpetually traipsing in and out to discuss all matters pertaining to the department, big or small, with Nanette. Nothing got through without first checking in with her and getting her approval. There were plush couches to sit in, bookcases filled to the brim with slim and thick paperbacks and hardcovers, comfy chairs to give rest to weary bodies, a nice view of Harvard Yard from the long and wide windows covering the far wall, and then Nanette's desk itself, made of steel cabinet "legs" and a heavy wooden panel balanced on top, immovable and permanent, with a white IBM/PC compatible perched in one corner and attached to it a dot-matrix printer. Nanette herself cut an imposing figure, despite her diminutive height and unbalanced gait, because she knew how to force a policy initiative down the Department's throat if she really wanted to, and everybody knew it. You definitely wanted her on your side.

"Hi Nanette, how are you?" I flashed her an embarrassed, goofy grin.

"Hello Jay, what can I do for you?" she replied, returning my grin with a toothy smile.

"I wanted to check up on the honors thesis requirements. What do I need to do or not do in order to write a senior thesis?" I enunciated for her.

"Well, young man, first of all, doing a thesis is entirely voluntary, with the only reservation being that the thesis-writer cannot be on academic probation, and that the project is on top of whatever for-credit courses you need to take in order to simply graduate."

"That's great news, ma'am! Well, I'm interested in the idea," I shared with Nanette, "and the lowest grade I have gotten to date is a B-."

"Well, then nothing should stop you!" she said in turn.

So that's how my senior year began to shape up, in ways and directions that I could never have imagined prior to embarking on the journey.

*****

In the meantime, as my mental faculties began to recover throughout junior summer, I didn't want to be reminded as much of the rave and club scene, which I had become somewhat weary of. One day I tracked Eliza down and we carried on a rambling conversation about classmates, courses, family and her roommate Liz.

"Eliza, I really like Liz, your roommate."

"But Jay, doesn't that mean that you were using me to get to her?" Eliza replied, initially hurt and confused.

"No, c'mon! We're friends. I wouldn't do that to you," I reassured her.

"Yeah, we're friends, I know. Do you want me to tell her?" Eliza said, recovering from the shock and now open to the idea.

Liz had left for California for the summer, and when she returned in her red Chevy coupe to campus towards the end of August, it was a happy reunion. I knew that Eliza had talked to Liz about my amorous intentions, because Liz had a ready giggle on her lips and a knowing look in her eye. Let's face it, folks: girls talk, in ways that are often way more intimate than how guys talk.

We set up a dinner date at a local Indian restaurant, and I remember the food was delicious, but more importantly I also remember one part of the conversation: Liz and I asking each other more than a couple times the question, "What exactly are you thinking right now?" That's when I suspected that some chemistry might exist between us, because I had asked her the same question moments previously. In my experience, in male-female conversation, the man usually rants, "Honey, try to see it my way!" and the woman typically complains, "Honey, don't tell me how I feel!"

I remember on a subsequent Friday night, as I was lying on my bed in my room, fantasizing about Liz, I decided to call her and see if she was available.

"Yo, what's up, Liz!" I shouted into the earpiece.

"Yeah Jay, what's up?" Liz responded, giggling back.

"What're you doing tonight?"

"I'm going to a party in Beacon Hill," she replied in a hushed voice. With that, I slammed the phone down on the receiver.

What had she meant? Did she mean that I was invited to a party with her in an ultra-exclusive part of Boston with social insiders and elites? Or was she reminding me of my place, and that my kind wasn't wanted around those parts? I hadn't stopped to confirm, but by hanging up the phone I had guessed that she meant the latter. From the first days of stepping onto Cambridge soil, I had totally dropped my cultural baggage. We were all at Harvard, after all; it didn't matter to me what others' particular backgrounds were, because I thought others didn't care about mine either. But the old conflicts between the clubbable and unclubbable, or the insiders versus the outsiders, hit me straight in the face as if someone had swung at me with a baseball bat. Being an Asian minority, being from the bourgeois middle-class, being from the gateway to the Midwest, being from new money, not being a WASP legacy, all those things…

The next Monday, I saw her in class in the lecture hall. Our gazes met, and she was apologetically inclined. We converged afterwards and walked away from the theater hall together.

"I don't think this is going to work out, Liz," I said to her, stopping for a moment to ruffle her golden hair and gaze straight into her eyes, as azure as the color of the sky on a clear summer's day.

"Jay…why can't we just hang out together?" she implored softly. I guess she meant in a pop-psychology way, as in "I'm OK, you're OK."

"Can't do it, hon." It was all I could do to pull off a weak smile.

"OK then," she turned and slowly walked away.

I just wasn't ready at that stage of college to stomach all our differences. They were too great. But this personal experience would prep me for the intellectual journey I was about to undertake, and that I would soon be one of the "Boston Brahmins" in my own unique way, maybe not as a generational legacy, nor because of my athletic prowess, but as an academic standout.

CHAPTER EIGHT

VIRTUE VERSUS THE PASSIONS

As senior year started in the fall of 1996, I did some cursory research and wrote a brief two-paragraph sketch about Kant's and Nietzsche's opposing philosophies. I then approached Professor Stanley, a very big name on campus and a very senior guy in the Philosophy Department, about meeting him in his office. The audacity on my part! I knew he'd be outside the Science Center's auditorium that evening because the schedule for his popular film class had been posted ahead of time. Still, he was a very tough guy to get a hold of; he was always surrounded by a crowd three or four deep. This time, though, I got to him in a brief temporary lull in the action.

Professor Stanley had a characteristically wide forehead below a bald pate that would make one think he carried an extra-large and well-honed brain. He was always dressed discreetly but prominently, as if to attract attention by his understatedness, which belied his fame on campus.

"Dr. Stanley, I would like to describe to you an idea I have for a senior honors thesis in philosophy. All I can say is that I think it is very interesting and I would learn a lot from it."

"Well, young man, since you're very enthusiastic, let's meet in Emerson 305 next Monday, say, 10 AM, as today is Friday and the weekend is upon us."

"Yes sir. I will be there."

So I was there, ten o'clock sharp on Monday morning, and Stanley was there, too, with his graduate student assistant, who nervously flitted around the office, taking orders from Stanley. He was wearing a tweed jacket and corduroy pants with an oxford blue dress shirt, with brown shoes. His office was sparsely decorated with books on shelves, no computer, black speckled linoleum hidden occasionally by Persian rugs and carpets. It was a little cold, and I was wearing just a T-shirt with baggy jeans and shoes. After he ordered his graduate student summarily to leave us, Stanley turned his attention to me.

"So! What do you have for me, young man? Let's hear this idea of yours!"

I began. "So we know that Kant's philosophy is rational, objective and disinterested, while Nietzsche's philosophy is emotional, subjective and partial. What if it were possible for these two philosophers' approaches to be melded into one in the same person, who would be civilized but natural, and would proceed not from a purely Kantian or purely Nietzschean philosophizing, but from a higher, synthesized level of philosophizing, which would consist of being open-minded and having standards at the same time?"

Now, naturally, all this was garbage, and I was probably still coming off my marijuana high from back at Adams House. However, to my damaged mind, the stuff was red hot, and apparently Stanley liked it, too!

"Jay, I think that is a wonderfully fascinating and incredibly interesting idea, and you should definitely pursue it through a thesis," he encouraged me, while staring off into space with a furrowed brow and drumming his thick fingers on his nearby desk. "Have you been assigned a thesis advisor yet?" he asked, now with a sense of urgency.

"No sir, I have not," I replied truthfully and honestly.

"See to it that you do, and make sure to ask Nanette the administrative head of the department to have me be your honors thesis advisor."

"Thank you, I will!"

Wow, this was amazing. A very senior member of the department had personally requested to be the advisor for my senior honors project. Wasn't that big? Buoyed by Stanley's response, and with a big cheese-eating grin on my face, I left his office in high spirits.

*****

I declared my intentions to Nanette, but apparently things didn't work out quite the way I had expected. Somebody else had been assigned to Stanley, and I was paired instead with Dr. Sally, a visiting professor from Dartmouth, not anybody permanent or senior in the department. In fact, she was not anybody I had heard of before, but still someone apparently quite knowledgeable about Kant and Nietzsche both, because she was teaching a course that semester on their contrasting conceptions of reason.

It was a bright summer-like day in September 1996 on Harvard's Cambridge campus. The weather was perfect; it couldn't have spelled more mental tranquility or spiritual calm. I had made an appointment to meet Professor Sally, my assigned tutor and mentor, about the senior honors thesis. My mood that day reminded me of the feeling I'd had four years ago in high school, in September 1992, when I asked the admissions representative on the phone if I had gotten into Harvard. Back then, the cicadas and the trees were hushed, and the ensuing developments showed that the whole universe, the world order, the entire cosmos, as it were, were looking down on me, this young man, and sending him off for the journey of a lifetime. Now, on this day in September

1996, four years later, the chirping of the birds in the yard, the rustling of the oaks and maples outside Emerson, and the cloudless blue sky up above, suggested through the senses yet another momentous occasion of the universe, the world, the cosmos—a sendoff on yet another journey. This time it would not be off and away to a distant place, but into the edge of within, into the mind's hidden recesses, brightly illuminated by the torch of enlightenment.

As I made my way up the stairs to her office on the third and highest floor of Emerson Hall, I felt pretty sure that I was onto something in my opening introductory statement, and that things would go smoothly. I had made numerous albeit minor changes to the material I had shown to Professor Stanley a week or so earlier.

"Professor Sally?" I peeked into her office.

"Oh, hi Jay!" she greeted me enthusiastically.

I was wearing my purple and yellow striped raver lid with a string tassel along with baggy jeans and a T-shirt, and I may have looked quite the cute "street urchin" to her.

Feeling self-important and more interested in getting down to business, I ignored the friendliness of her greeting as I made myself comfortable in one of her office chairs. Somewhat taken aback by my no-nonsense attitude, she made casual small talk briefly, and then let me push forward. I read my opening statement out loud, and fell silent to hear her response.

"So what do you think?" I asked with smug confidence, feeling that I had bowled her over with the genius of my work. I was expecting a good reception, the way Dr. Stanley had responded.

Professor Sally, having recovered from my rebuff, stridently replied, "Well, Jay, it's very rough."

"I know, I know," I superficially agreed, feeling utterly deflated underneath the outwardly stolid mask of deference. I must have flinched visibly, because I felt as if I had just been smacked dead in the face by a solid moving brick wall. My face froze as I tried to maintain my composure, while my eyes watered up with tears. After all that effort and time spent on refining two paragraphs of writing for Professor Stanley, who loved it, she was telling me the opposite, that it wasn't up to par? My ego was bruised; I guess I was mad, but it was more as if I were wounded. This was going to be a pretty tough nut to crack, but at least my overreaction showed how much I cared about what I was doing.

"Now then, exactly what distinction between Kant's and Nietzsche's moral philosophies do you refer to?"

I trailed off, my mouth wide open, trying to vocalize and match words to my inchoate, churning thoughts. Baffled and unnerved by my own incoherence, at how vulnerable I was to the Professor's sharp and intelligent probing, I yelped, "I don't know, Professor, this is very difficult!"

"Well, I know it is, young man! And I would not be your teacher if that were not so," she replied quietly, ever the benevolent master. "But if you're not able to identify the essential conflict you seem to sense between these two thinkers, you cannot proceed with writing a thesis. So please try again."

Downcast, and disturbed by how hard this apparently was going to be, but still not out for the count just yet, I met her kind, smiling gaze.

"OK Professor. I'll try again."

*****

I struggled with the paltry Introduction for almost four months, between the September meeting with Professor Sally and her final vote of approval during December's winter break. First I had to get out of the deep hole of my drug-induced haze before I could put together sentences, and then from there, move up far above ground to put together paragraphs. That's why the Introduction took so long, even though it was only two pages, because so much needed to go into it while so much impairment existed. But all the while Sally helped me to get the ball rolling.

Looking back, I also realize the initial error of my ways: I kept trying to do something brand spanking new, to reinvent the wheel, as it were. I kept taking notes and copying word-for-word passages from both philosophers' writings, which forced me to confront the meaning of their texts. After two months of undeniable progress during which I became intimately familiar with

Kant and Nietzsche, but also had inefficiently expended much effort because I couldn't coherently organize my thoughts, Professor Sally gave me a bit of advice in a meeting of ours in late October, around Halloween.

"Jay, it is enough simply to convey the magnitude and extent of the problem; you do not have to do anything new. Try," she went on, "to find a passage from the works of Kant and Nietzsche that encapsulates each philosopher's overall *gestalt* that will be the kernel of your thesis."

"OK Professor, I'll do that." I hung onto that advice, because I knew that on my own I was grasping at straws and coming up short. I felt reinvigorated with a renewed sense of purpose and direction and left her office, once more upbeat and ready for the challenge.

I began to explore the texts that I had used for Arata's and David's seminars. I also began to focus on specific texts: the *Grounding for the Metaphysics of Morals* for Kant, and *The Antichrist* for Nietzsche. I kept looking in these two slim volumes, back and forth between the two, before I realized that Kant's objective and formal quote would have to come first, and then Nietzsche's vicious, impassioned repartee would come second, as if in response, and also in the sequence that I had been exposed to the two: Kant in sophomore year, Nietzsche in junior year. So this was what I came up with, and this was ultimately what I settled upon:

"Innocence is indeed a glorious thing; but unfortunately it does not keep very well and is easily led astray. Consequently, even wisdom, which consists more in doing and not doing than in knowing – needs science, not in order to learn from it, but in order that wisdom's precepts may gain acceptance and permanence. Man feels within himself a powerful counterweight to all the commands of duty, which are presented to him by reason as so pre-eminently worthy of respect. This counterweight consists of all his needs and inclinations, whose total satisfaction is summed up under the name of happiness. Now reason irremissibly commands its precepts, without thereby promising the inclinations anything; hence it disregards and neglects these impetuous and at the same time so seemingly plausible claims (which do not allow themselves to be suppressed by any command)."

– Immanuel Kant, Grounding for the Metaphysics of Morals

"An action demanded by the instinct of life is proved to be right by the pleasure that accompanies it; yet this nihilist with his Christian dogmatic entrails considered pleasure an objection. What could destroy us more quickly than working, thinking, and feeling without any inner necessity, without any deeply personal choice, without pleasure – as an automaton of 'duty?' This is the very recipe for decadence, even for idiocy. Kant became an idiot. And this man was a contemporary of Goethe! This catastrophic spider was considered the German

philosopher – he still is! I beware of saying what I think of the Germans."

– Friedrich Nietzsche, The Antichrist

The Introduction began with these two quotes juxtaposed next to each other, Kant's first and at the top, and then Nietzsche's second and below. And as part of the Introduction, I included a two-page discussion of these two quotes.

The understanding of Kant that comes from his quote is that our rational faculty is a source of moral knowledge that is independent of and superior to the five senses. For Nietzsche, however, the basic understanding of him is that the opposite of reason, that is, the biological, instinctual and emotional drives in all human beings, is the seat and source of moral conviction. With these two diametrically opposite and seemingly irreconcilable philosophical worldviews juxtaposed next to each other, I set in motion a duality universal to all the world's great religions and ancient philosophies: Virtue vs. the Passions, and their analogues, Reason vs. Emotion, Thought vs. Feeling, and the modern derivatives, Cognition vs. Affect.

What was at real stake here for me was that the Head and the Heart needed to be united if I could properly be possessed of wisdom. The idea of "freedom"—not liberal democratic freedom, as in doing what you want, with whomever you want, wherever you want, whenever you want—but as specifically a moral freedom entailing responsibility, came to me as part of the thesis idea. That is, if I were to be truly "free," as in self-determining and autonomous, then I must think impartially as well as feel committedly, together. Ultimately, the title of the thesis began to take shape into a finished form somewhere around this time: *Kant and Nietzsche on Virtue and the Passions: Thoughts on their Conceptions of Freedom.*

"OK, so Jay, you want to focus on Virtue and the Passions for Kant and Nietzsche. If that is the case, then you have to ask yourself what Virtue looks like to Kant and to Nietzsche?"

"Well Professor, I think that if we are talking about Virtue for Kant and for Nietzsche, then we have to identify their ethical ideals. And Kant's ethical ideal is his so-called *good will,* and Nietzsche's ethical ideal is his so-called *übermensch.*"

"Good Jay, that's fine. But is Kant's *good will* and Nietzsche's *übermensch* equal to each other in temperament? Or are they diametrically opposed?"

"Well, clearly Nietzsche and Kant are opposed to each other morally speaking, but I am also arguing for a commonality. So I would have to say that I am doing a comparison and contrast of Kant and Nietzsche's ethical ideals."

"OK, so get it down on paper and start shaping up the argument," Sally said as she dismissed me. So between Halloween and Christmas the Introduction was fine-tuned.

Professor Sedgwick finally emailed me the following missive during the holiday break:

Hi Jay,

I read your introduction, and now it is in sufficiently good shape for you to continue forward.

At this point, you have got to start writing as soon and as quickly as possible. I am simply not encouraged by how little time you have left to finish the thesis by the submission date in April.

Let us set up a date and time to meet in the New Year when you return to Cambridge to discuss plans for your project.

Happy holidays,
Prof. S.

I felt alternately hopeful and discouraged by her email. Here I was trying to churn out as much material as possible in as little time as possible, and there I was told that I was barely getting by. But then again, shit flows downstream, and I wasn't about to question her authority in my reply.

Dear Professor,

Thank you for your email. I look forward to seeing you in January when I return.

Sincerely,
Jay

So with my ego still sorely bruised, but hopes not entirely dashed, I returned to the cold, snow and wind of Cambridge in January 1997 prepared to proceed once more "unto the breach."

*****

From January 1997 to the following April, my habits completely changed. I fell off the party scene, which died down considerably once I focused on my work. After all, I had been the main proponent of the party life in my roommates' neck of the woods, and now they started to leave on Friday and Saturday nights for other parts of campus, such as Dunster House closer by the Charles River where other kindred party spirits existed, or simply to other parts of Adams House, where ongoing drugging and drinking continued unabated, with or without me. I began to eat meals alone in the cafeteria, tiring easily of company and preoccupied with philosophical musings in my mind or imagining how to structure the latest paragraph in progress. I even became somewhat antisocial and belligerent, rather irritably determined to overcome and erase the hilarity-ensuing "dancing clown" image I had portrayed at rave parties. I started living in the library, checking out the maximum 50 volumes at a time, sitting on the floor to get to the lower-placed paperbacks, reaching on tippy-toe to snag the higher-placed hardcovers, and exploring the secondary readings and commentaries on Kant and Nietzsche. My personal hygiene, which had been well-maintained to impress members of the opposite sex, began to head south; beard-shaving and teeth-brushing became too time-consuming and labor-intensive to bother with. I was so intensely preoccupied that even a much-needed five minute shower seemed too much of a waste of time away from writing and reading. My personal appearance also began to deteriorate. My head, which had been shaved since sophomore year, slowly began to sprout greasy, unkempt locks of hair. Dark circles from fatigue, stress and overexertion slowly appeared prominently around my eyes. I was constantly awake on four, maybe five hours of sleep at most, and eating became a chore, not a pleasure. I lost weight, down another 10 pounds to 145 on my now disturbingly rail-thin 5'9" frame. My brow was constantly furrowed with deep and knotted thoughts. My breath was bad and a pungent body odor began to trail me wherever I walked.

But all this came with one redeeming quality: I had completely stopped the drugs. With the exception of coffee, cigarettes, and the occasional alcoholic drink, I became straightedge, which was really the only way to be for someone who was putting his mind in overdrive

24/7. Indeed, it was almost easy to quit, because my wits had been so addled, and I had hit such rock-bottom. So there was no way to go but up.

However, the writing wasn't coming along well. I would meet with Professor Sally periodically, and she would constantly remind me that the writing needed vast improvements in structure, logic and coherence. She would point out remedial deficiencies like faulty syntax, overused vocabulary, and excessive punctuation ("You use the semicolon too much.").

"Now I warned you about this, Jay, but since you were so 'determined' to do a thesis, I decided to let you have the opportunity," she said as she farcically gestured with her clenched fists.

I became the eternally optimistic pupil to the erudite master ever so the Jeremiah about the student's chances of achieving intellectual maturity. I kept popping up, all confident and replete with the latest paragraph or pages I had written, only for Professor Sally to mow me down with her criticisms. It was if I would put up tenpins and she would promptly knock them down. It was complete and utter ego-destruction, a lesson in total frustration. Nothing was ever good enough for her. And I was subjecting myself to this voluntarily! Who in their right mind would undergo this sort of torture willingly?

The straw that broke the camel's back fell in mid-March, after two and a half months of fighting against all odds. Sally emailed the following:

Hello Jay,

I am afraid that I do not see you receiving honors if you continue at the present trajectory. There is not much more I can do for you, other than to warn you that your efforts will be in vain. I urge you to consider my advice, and make a final decision to terminate this project now.

I am sorry I cannot bear you better news at this time.

Prof. S.

Utterly rattled, I thought the implications through. If I quit, as she suggested, then all the effort up to that point would be wasted. But if I went through with the project, chances were I would not receive *cum laude* after my name, so the original goal would never be achieved. A veritable "no-win scenario" with no effective resolution, like the Kobayashi Maru scenario in Star Trek II: The Wrath of Khan, but certainly a noble test of character. At that point, I decided to make an appointment to meet with Nanette to inform her of my decision.

"Hi Nanette," I spoke up, downcast and downtrodden, but with a pale smile on my face.

"Hello Jay, what can I do for you?" Nanette queried. That day, her desk looked bigger and wider and more covered with tomes than ever.

"Well, it's something about my thesis. Professor Sally stated that she really didn't think that I should continue with the project, since chances are I won't get honors upon graduation."

"So that's what she said? I see. OK, then what do you want to do?"

"Well, I would like to proceed forward with the thesis, and it doesn't matter to me whether or not I receive honors for it, because I am learning so much. I would like to continue working on the project—for its own sake." This was straight from the heart.

"For its own sake, Jay? Hmmm…" Nanette stared directly at me with a far-off, half-lidded gaze, inscrutable behind thick glasses. It was as if she were thinking something in the back of her mind, and also not just looking at me, but rather looking into me and through me. "OK Jay, for its own sake, eh? I will inform the department about your decision."

"Thank you, Nanette. Have a nice day."

"Good-bye, young man."

The conversation took less than two minutes.

Now I don't know exactly what was said between the administrative office and the department, or what exactly was discussed between Nanette and Professor Sally, but apparently word got around about what I had told Nanette. When I met with Professor Sally the next time after that, there was a complete 180-degree change in her attitude that could not have been attributed entirely to the progress I had made since the last revision of the manuscript.

"Well Jay, I think you should be able to receive at least with honors, based on the progress I've seen."

"Thank you, Professor," I said quietly and thankfully acknowledging her compliment. I did not want to reveal my churning feelings of joy, relief and, yes, utter and complete exhaustion as I left her office that late March day.

*****

Soon after that meeting with Professor Sally, I returned to WHRB-FM 95.3's DJ studio on a Tuesday morning at 11 AM. I selected for performance the following playlist:

1. Quincy Jones Orchestra – "The Quintessence"
2. Ben Webster and Harry "Sweets" Edison – "My Romance"
3. Sarah Vaughan – "Come Rain or Come Shine"
4. Roy Hargrove Quintet – "Everything I Have (Dedicated to You)"
5. John Coltrane Quartet – "You Don't Know What Love Is"
6. Stanley Turrentine – "Someone to Watch Over Me"
7. Dinah Washington – "Teach Me Tonight"
8. Yusef Lateef Quartet – "In the Evening"
9. John Coltrane Quartet – "My Favorite Things"
10. Charlie Haden Quartet West – "Every Time We Say Good-bye"

Both phone lines started blinking immediately. *Oh, no, here we go again...*

"WHRB Harvard Radio."

"Excuse me, are you the DJ?" a man asked.

"Yes, I am. How can I help you?" I responded cautiously, not sure whether this was going to be a complaint or compliment.

"Please send me one of your playlists. I have not heard programming this good in a very long time," he said, apparently deeply impressed.

"Yes, sir. Please give me your address." I was trembling. I felt so vindicated by this feedback. *There, take that, Nate, you fucker!* After three years of sticking to it, I now knew a lot about jazz, what forms I liked (ballad), what subgenres I liked (female vocals) and what instruments I liked (alto and tenor saxophones)…as well as what I didn't like (fusion and free jazz). But it was more than just knowing jazz; it was about having a taste for it, or perhaps more accurately, having good taste in it. The lines kept buzzing…

"WHRB-FM 95.3, how can I help you?"

"Hey, uh, you the DJ?" someone else inquired.

"Yes, what's up, man," I said, reverting to street slang, and again cautious about the reception.

"Hey man, you know that stuff you were playing, John Coltrane, Ben Webster? You know, I grew up with those guys, man, I GREW UP with them! Even when I was IN JAIL I was still listening to that stuff, they couldn't keep me down, man!"

"Man, that's an amazing story, my friend. Thank you so much for sharing that with me."

"Yeah, so, uh, you know, when do you have your DJ time, because I tell you what, man, sometimes when I'm listening to those other DJs on your radio station, I just gotta turn it off, man, you know? I just gotta turn it off, 'cause they don't know what to play, that ain't jazz, you know."

"Hey man, I'm here every Tuesday morning and afternoon from 11 AM to 1 PM. My name is Jay, and you can always catch me then!"

"Alright, Jay, my name's Walter. Thanks again!"

*****

I returned to my cubbyhole mailbox toward the waning days of senior spring, and in it there was a small off-white colored card on elegant stationery, shaped like a thank-you note, with some text on the inside, and a self-addressed stamped return envelope for the Harvard Varsity Club. Well, what do you know? I knew I had been invited a couple times before in just as many years, and at both times I had passed up on the offer—once out of innocent disregard, the second time out of cross indignation. But this time was different. I took it with me to the cafeteria and sat down with my food, all the while inspecting the contents of the envelope to make sure nothing else was included.

Smurfy had spied me as he ran down the steps to grab lunch, and he sat down next to me at one of those long wooden tables in the Adams House cafeteria.

"Hey Smurfy…I got an invitation to be a member of the Harvard Varsity Club."

"Really?" he asked, astonished. He leaned over to take a look at what was in my hand.

"Yeah, it's the third time in as many years that they've asked me."

"Well, better late than never, Jay," Smurfy muttered, looking floored. "Do you know that some guys fight like all fucking hell over that stuff? Everybody in my boat wanted to get in there." Smurfy was a varsity coxswain on men's crew, so he knew how competitive things could get at the varsity level. And here I was, never having gotten past the freshman level of participation in lacrosse, and yet constantly vetted for years, despite my indecision to sign up for this shining privilege.

"Alright, I'll do it," I declared, more to myself than to Smurfy. I realized then that my freshman year teammates had been pulling for me to "join the club," so to speak, for no other reason than out of appreciation for my contribution to the team and to the organization. They had come to me in friendship for three years, and for three years I had pushed them away. Well, not anymore. I pulled out a pen and checked the box signaling my consent and interest, and got up from my lunch to deposit the self-addressed stamped return envelope in the nearest mail slot.

CHAPTER NINE

EVERYTIME WE SAY GOOD-BYE

I submitted the finished thesis in late April 1997, a few weeks after the last meeting with Professor Sally. I remember running to Kinko's to have the document professionally printed on 3-ring, heavy bond paper, all five copies, one for each of the three committee members, one for myself, and one for the department. I could smell my own body odor and tried to smooth over my greasy, overgrown hair as I waited for my order number to be called by the clerk. All 56 pages slid inside a black 3-ring binder with the cover page containing the title, author name and submission requirements.

I sprinted from the Kinko's in Harvard Square to Nannette's office on the third floor of Emerson Hall.

"Nanette, I throw myself at your feet for mercy's sake!"

She chuckled and gathered the information and documents she would need ready for the committee: the four copies, not including my own.

"Well done, young man! Now get some sleep and I'll do the rest."

Afterwards, I didn't feel any different. No weight of the world lifted from my shoulders, no blinding joy from a remarkable feat accomplished. Just world-weariness, a desire to rest my head on a pillow, and just lie down, cradling my overtaxed and overspent brain.

Nevertheless, in May, I was called upon to defend my thesis orally in front of the Dissertation Committee. I showered reluctantly, donned a short-sleeve polo shirt and jeans with a pair of brown Doc Maarten oxfords, and trudged on over to Emerson Hall. Climbing the steps to the third floor and shuffling to just outside the main conference room, I met Nanette. Mind you, the guy after me who was defending his thesis wore a navy sack suit, and I probably should have worn at least a blazer and slacks over a dress shirt.

The door opened, and Sally said, "We're ready for you now," as she motioned me in, a reserved smile on her face.

I put my biggest smile forward and offered a kind greeting. "Good morning, Professors."

There were three faculty members there: Stanley, Sally and Richard, who was an associate professor at the time. Stanley was the most senior as a chaired professor but was on the verge of retirement, while Sally was the visiting assistant professor and lowest in rank.

The windows looked outside into the greenery of the oaks and maples planted next to Emerson Hall. The room was air-conditioned and comfortable, despite the heat of a New England May. A large wooden conference table consisting of smaller wooden tables rested prominently in the center of the room, around which the professors sat. I was shown to the head of the table and into a black plastic seated and shiny steel framed chair.

Stanley wore a herringbone blazer and richly colored blue dress shirt with a slightly crumpled yellow tie, still fashionable for an older gentleman. Richard wore a grey blazer with an oxford blue button-down shirt, the perfect uniform for his position. And Sally wore an ivory linen two-piece jacket and pants that worked well with the dark green shirt blouse she wore underneath. All in all, all three dressed conservatively but not in a dull way. And I felt immediately comfortable and at ease in their presence.

"So Jay, we think your project is quite remarkable and you have broached a very interesting topic," Richard intoned.

"Well, I should say, sir, that as Professor Sally mentioned to me, it is enough simply to convey the magnitude and extent of the problem. I don't have to do anything new," I replied steadily and with a respectful nod to Sally at the side of the table.

"Well Jay, I think you have done something new here," Richard corrected me gently. At that moment, I felt sure about myself and trusted that these professors would allow me to be emotionally vulnerable and not take advantage of any weaknesses I might display.

Then the discussion switched to Stanley. "Mr. Kim, Kant is a very eminent philosopher, and you focus on the Kantian 'inclination,' which has been the subject of countless PhD dissertations, let alone undergraduate theses. To your point, how would you describe your interpretation of the Kantian inclination to us?"

I knew then that he was trying to gently motivate me to articulate my own particular views. We went back and forth about this for a good 30 minutes, until, when he offered an example of a Kantian inclination to me based on his understanding of my definition, I adamantly declared, "No! That is not a correct definition of the term, inclination!"

Stanley immediately jumped up in his seat, his heavy frame elevating, his bald pate shining, his furrowed brow loosening, and responded with benevolent righteousness, "And you're the Mother and I'm the Child!"

To this I could only laugh embarrassedly, my newcomer bullheadedness in sharp contrast to his mature, gentle overtures of tolerance and acceptance. It really was a magical moment: an initiation rite conducted by a wizened wolf for a young upstart champing at the bit.

After that repartee, and nearly an hour and 15 minutes after the commencement of the defense, Sally intoned, "OK Jay, the committee now has enough information to assess your candidacy for honors. We will get in touch with you in the next two weeks, in time for your commencement ceremony and graduation day."

"Thank you, Professor. Have a good day, all of you!" I grinned, as I got up out of my seat and headed for the door.

Trailing me, Sally replied, "We hope you have a chance to relax a bit and enjoy the rest of the semester, Jay."

About two weeks afterwards, I received a handwritten note from Nanette on behalf of the Dissertation Committee, containing the comments of Professor Richard on my work, as well as the final decision of the Committee regarding my honors status. Richard went into rather involved detail about various issues dealing with the writing, but his only major complaint, which could have been taken as a good one, was that he would have liked me to have "taken the work much further" than what I had accomplished. Apparently he was interested in my topic and thought there would be merit in expanding it at a future time. Professor Sally did not have any notes, given that she was my advisor and knew the work more intimately than either Stanley or Richard. Professor Stanley himself wrote nothing as well, but for a different reason, according to Nanette. He was about to retire after a very long 40-year career, so he could be rightfully excused from performing any more final swan songs. I gritted my teeth and nodded to Nanette.

In any case, the decision of the Committee was that the written text was a *magna cum laude* (with high honors) while the oral defense was *cum laude* (with honors), and so after further deliberation, they decided to give me *cum laude*. So again I swallowed my pride and forced myself away from picking fights with anybody in the department over this nicety. And so that was it. At that moment, I was completely "burnt out."

*****

Shortly afterwards, Eliza came to see me. I greeted her in my customary over-excited tenor, which she played along with for a while as we walked up to the room suite.

We sat down on near-opposite sides of the comfortable L-shaped couch. Then Eliza's cheerful gaze fell, and my own chirpy smile and overjoyed countenance vanished.

"Jay, that's amazing how you wrote your thesis. I'm so impressed. I, seriously, I could never do something like that. I just can't, it's not in me," she said as she stared off into space, and then at me in earnest awe. I almost was going to tell her cheerfully to her face that anybody can accomplish such a feat, when my dark depression and angry irritability both enveloped me like a rising tide at sea. Right at the point when college was about to end, these feelings started to surface unpredictably. Something was wrong.

"Jay, it's really tough when a person has a shitty family to deal with, and I guess there are evil people at Harvard, too," she started off, revealing some of her inner torment. I was mystified by her opening remark, not sure how it managed to be relevant to me. But then she started talking about her father, how much of a tyrant and boor he was, how he would sacrifice the family's security to gratify his needs.

"Yeah, Jay, one time my father ordered the whole rest of the family to stay in the car a whole night on a vacation trip while he registered a hotel room for himself." At the time, I didn't know how what she was saying applied to any other family but hers. However, she apparently had a sixth sense about these things, and she simply might have picked up on the flawed nature of the father-son relationship in my family.

"Jay, you know, it's a lot better if you just open up and don't keep it all bottled up inside," Eliza pleaded desperately with me, as I sat there with a big, ugly brown frown on my face. Everybody around me knew that something was wrong, and I couldn't hide it anymore. Even so, I kept putting up walls. I wouldn't confess my real emotional issues to anybody.

Eliza continued. "You know, I was with this one guy recently. I…, uh, I used him. I exploited him and manipulated him. He was weak and vulnerable, and I got him to do what I wanted him to do." That got my attention, as I had never seen this serious self-reflective side of Eliza, only the irresponsible party side. Here was a potential opening, a chance to vent my own emotional and interpersonal frustrations with someone whom I trusted. I seriously wanted to sit in her lap and start crying. But I sat still and silent by myself, as the depression and anger reappeared on my face and inside my mind.

I continued to give Eliza a mean, unhappy look, which prompted her to say, “Well, at least I tried.” She rose from her seat and headed for the door. Stopping for a moment and looking back, she asked, “Jay, do you want the rest of my pot?” It seemed to be an earnest final parting gift.

In a final gesture of kindness, I declined, “No, you keep it for yourself,” and then I accompanied her downstairs to the outer door, as we said our final good-bye’s.

*****

A few hours after the encounter with Eliza, I felt my irritability subside substantially. Seeking renewed reconciliation and sustained rapport, I called the number for her room. Instead of Eliza, Liz picked up.

“Hey, Jay, congratulations!” Liz carried on, obviously having heard of the positive turnout of the thesis. “How’s it feel?” she inquired.

“It feels fine,” I responded in a monotone.

“Hey, that’s really incredible, none of my girlfriends got honors, you know…” she giggled good-naturedly.

“Thanks a lot, Liz,” my voice sounded tired at least to me.

"So there's not much going on right now, you should come over and hang out, you know?" Yeah, I know, sure, I know…

"OK, so, can you just tell Eliza I said hi?" I shunted Liz aside.

"What?!" she exclaimed. "OK, take care, Jay," Liz ended, her voice hushed by concern and pain.

"Alright," I closed, and that was the last I ever heard of her.

*****

Along with the visit from Eliza, I instinctively reached out to Aidan after the completion of the thesis. I thought that she might have a perspective on what was going on with me.

"Aidan!" I said loudly into the mouthpiece of the cordless phone.

"Yeah Jay, I can hear you," she laughed cheerfully.

"Aidan, I'm telling you, I don't know what's going on with me!" I rattled off.

"What's the matter, Jay?" Aidan asked, incredulous upon hearing this insecure, inadequate Jay for the first time.

"I'm so Goddamn competitive, I just can't stop thinking about outdoing other people!" I panted into the phone, giving free rein to the pent-up emotions locked inside me. Looking back, I now know what was wrong. What had worked for my father, his ultra-competitive spirit and the satisfaction he took with feeling that he was better than his vanquished professional foes, had been internalized inside of me and passed down from father to son. But now the suitability of that psychology was being tested, as I voiced my very real discomfort with what I was now feeling: all burnt out. I told her, "All that competitiveness has left me feeling exhausted!"

"I don't know what to say, Jay, I don't know!" Aidan exclaimed in a suddenly worried and anxiety-ridden tone of voice. "Jay, what's going on? Did something happen?"

"Well, I don't know what to do! Do you?"

"Jay, look, why don't you try some therapy and medication, sweetheart? That's what worked for me." So again, here was a confession, another opening for me, a literal invitation to get some help in the way that Aidan specifically knew could work, just as how Eliza had opened up to me previously, basically pleading with me not to let my problems stay all bottled up inside. But again, I refused the offer.

"Yeah, but surely you must have seen something about me that makes me so competitive, Aidan!"

"Jay, I'm sorry, but I didn't see this coming…I really didn't. Are you sure you're going to be OK?"

"Yeah, I'll be alright," I said, hanging up the phones after saying our good-byes.

Smurfy emerged from his own room, smiling disingenuously and joyfully quipping, "You know, Jay, if that's how she's making you feel, it's probably not what you want!" He'd apparently been eavesdropping. Irritated by his flippant remark, I retreated into my room and slammed the door behind me. I needed to be alone for a while.

*****

I had gone to the nightclubs around the time I had submitted my thesis formally, to let loose some steam, but I wasn't feeling well at all. My moods see-sawed between enraged irritability to abject depression, and back. The scene which I had grown to love became a place of aversion. Then, from the crowd of anonymous partyers, Amian emerged and approached me, mouthing unexpected words silently: "I love you!" What did she say? That she loves me? I was elated! I was so excited! That lifted my spirits tremendously! No girl that I had been interested in had ever expressed her true feelings to me so openly. Amian and I smiled back and forth at each other, and then she shouted into my ear that she was leaving the club.

I called her the very next day, and asked her to do coffee—to which she agreed. Later that day, we sat down in the outer patio of a Starbucks in Harvard Square, where I bought her drink and mine. Coffee it is! We started talking.

"So Amian, I'm so happy about what you told me last night."

"What did I tell you last night?" she asked, looking up while slurping her coffee.

"You know! That you love me?" I had thrown my cards on the table. I smiled and giggled.

Her wide brown eyes suddenly darted at me and squinted shiftily.

"Jay, what are you talking about?"

"Aren't you in love with me? I thought you told me that back at the club last night?"

"Jay, I didn't say that! Wait, you thought I said I loved you?"

"Well, didn't you?" I asked indignantly, starting to feel uncomfortable. Her eyes unsquinted and began to get bug-eyed. My smile froze.

"Jay, I asked you if you were ALRIGHT… Jay, I'm IN a relationship! I'm INVOLVED with someone right now… Jay, you never ever tell me what's on your mind. I have no idea what's going on with you…Jesus Christ, Jay, you actually imagined that I said that, and then you convinced yourself that I said it?"

Amian rose up from her seat, her voice rising to near hysteria: "Oh my God, Jay, you just DELUDED yourself! You are in a state of delusion! OH MY FUCKING GOD, Jay, get a grip!" She tore away from the coffee table and hurried away back to campus. I was left sitting there alone as coffee dribbled from my lips onto the front of my shirt.

Later that night, my roommates fielded a phone call from Amian. I had been lying on the couch, cradling my head on my arms, trying to make sense of what had just happened earlier at the café. I was terrified that I was losing my grip on reality, that there was no way to justify my line of thinking. Fearful of what Amian might say, I raised the phone to my head with great apprehension.

"Hello?" I queried weakly.

"Jay? It's Amian."

"Hey, there…"

"Jay, did you think about what I said earlier?"

"Yeah, Amian, I've been trying to relax a bit and just chill for a sec."

"Jay, do you want to come over and talk about it? Like right now?"

"Uh, you know, I'm just gonna lie down here in my room for a little bit longer. I think that's what I need."

"OK, Jay, you sure?" she cautioned.

"Yes, I'm sure."

"OK, then, I'll talk to you later."

"Sounds good," I said, putting the phone back on the receiver.

This was narcissism and erotomania. I had enshrouded myself in the lie and felt perfectly content to do so, until Amian dispelled it abruptly. Again, I needed help, more help than anybody around me could do for me themselves.

*****

Last rave, last hour.

Still reeling from the encounter with Amian, I went on my last rave of my college career. It would also be my last college XTC trip.

I ingested the pill from an anonymous drug dealer, not Sam this time, and who knows what shit was cut into it. I started feeling woozy and out of place. I tried dancing, but I had fallen into a cesspool of abject dejection. Someone was taking pictures of the Harvard group that had made it to the rave; I teetered on the outskirts of the frame. I felt an impending sense of doom take over. The feeling was similar to what I had experienced two years earlier, when Kee and I felt the acid trip we were on together start to take over and destructively infiltrate our minds. Only this time it wasn't a thought in my head, but a feeling in my heart.

I tried to have fun, but couldn't. The rave was located at an abandoned, cleared-out hockey rink, and it was all I could do to sit on the bleachers and not put my head in my hands. The house beat pounded through into my head and reverberated inside, much like a .22 caliber bullet that had entered the skull of a shooting victim and was bouncing around back and forth inside, careening off the walls of the cranium. This torture went on for hours…

Finally, as if the wait were worth it, my Harvard group was leaving. I had driven to the rave in my station wagon, and now people were piling in, including Amian and Aidan. We all fastened our seat belts and started off on the journey back to Harvard Square.

Again, something was wrong with me. It was almost as if I were having a horrifying epiphany while I was driving. I felt completely worthless, helpless and hopeless. Meanwhile, something was telling me, "People have been trying to help you. You have no value on your own whatsoever, unless it's through other people, whether friends, family or teachers. Jay, your life is over, you are a complete and total zero…"

I started pulling over to the side of the road, an area which contained nothing but loamy grass and weeds, extremely bumpy terrain. As I slowed to a non-freeway speed, my hands on the wheel became masterless. I swerved to the extreme left and to the extreme right, back and forth, while my passengers cried out in alarm. The car tipped dangerously on two wheels from my choppy movements on the steering wheel.

"Whoa Jay, take it easy!" was all I could hear from Amian (or was it Aidan?) in a surreal ordinariness of voice. They were too frightened even to scream out their terror and horror at what was transpiring and seemed to be spiraling out of control. For 30 seconds, I kept swerving back and forth, accelerating, never decelerating, sometimes pumping the brakes to come closer to the tipping point. Everybody in the car was quietly but audibly carrying on, knowing that I had them trapped as prisoners, and that anything self-destructive I did to myself and the car would also happen to them. It was my first near-death encounter, not from a danger located outside, but from suicidal urges emerging inside.

Then, after 30 seconds, the moment passed. My cognitions disappeared, my affect receded, and I regained control of the steering wheel. Getting back on the road, we headed back to Harvard Square without further incident. For the entire rest of the journey, everybody in the car was completely silent. Upon arrival, everybody emptied out, scurrying for their respective destinations on campus. I went to my room and just lay there on the mattress, feigning sleep. That last rave of my college career was quite a let-down from my beginnings three years before in this fast party scene. "Burnt out" from the academic scene, I had completely "fallen off" the party scene.

*****

On June 5, 1997, I sat with my parents and brother happily surrounding me, my black cap and gown generously covering my tall, skinny frame. We were waiting in the inside courtyard of Adams House, ready for me to walk up and receive my diploma. The House Master called student residents' names one by one, and then he said mine. I pulled myself together for the formal walk up to the podium. I mustered a wan smile, shook the House Master's hand, and received my diploma in my outstretched arms. I was curious to see it, and because it was unframed, in a manila folder, I was able to peek inside:

HARVARD UNIVERSITY
AT CAMBRIDGE IN THE COMMONWEALTH OF MASSACHUSETTS

The President and Fellows of Harvard College, with the consent of the Honorable and Reverend Board of Overseers and acting on the recommendation of the Faculty of Arts and Sciences,

have conferred on
JAY HAWK KIM
the degree of Bachelor of Arts
Cum Laude in Philosophy.

In witness whereof, by authority duly committed to us, we have hereunder placed our names and the seal of the University on this fifth day of June in the Year of Our Lord nineteen hundred and ninety-seven and of Harvard College the three hundred and sixty-first.

N.L. RUDENSTINE, PRESIDENT
H.R. LEWIS, DEAN OF THE COLLEGE
J.R. KNOWLES, DEAN OF THE FACULTY
R.J. KIELY, MASTER OF ADAMS HOUSE

It was anticlimactic, having worked so hard and come so far in eight months, and then the ultimate difference being two extra words—*Cum Laude*—placed after your degree and name.

In the ensuing days that family was visiting, my upperclassmen roommates who got into Adams House with me gave me a send-off. Kee and I embraced; he would have to be at Harvard for one more year before graduating, and I took pity on his plight. Smurfy gave me an awed, stone-faced handshake; he still couldn't figure out how I had pulled off the senior honors thesis, and he never knew that he had gotten into the upperclassmen rooming group for Adams House three and a half years ago by the slimmest of margins, solely because of my and Jerseyboy's good graces. As for Jerseyboy, I shook his hand, bear-hugged him and gave him a knowing look, which he reciprocated, as if we were saying to each other, "You were a real pleasure to be with, I enjoyed your company very much, and I will remember you quite fondly. Oh, and sorry about Smurfy!"

I wasn't planning to say good-bye to Sam, "the tutor and feeder of my riots," as it were. He was to be abandoned by everybody he had hung out with on campus. Without an internal moral compass congruent with his acquired pedigree, his degree was a dead letter, a moldy sheepskin rotted through-and-through. Everybody had just kept him around because he brought good drugs, and everybody knew in turn that Sam had tried to control us with his little arsenal of "medications." Still—and I remember this very vividly—he and I spied each other out after the individual House graduation ceremonies, along one of the many cobblestone sidewalks lining the campus, both of us wearing our black caps and gowns, looking equally dignified on the outside but revealing none of the inequity in moral fiber on the inside, and from a distance I gave him a big cheese-eating grin, knowing that I had finally overcome his unholy influence on me. He returned a bemused smile, as if to ask, "Jay, we're buddies, why won't you say good-bye to me?" But there would be no hugs or handshakes, no final salutations, just my heading for the West Coast and leaving New England behind. I had a job waiting for me at a top-20 law firm, Irell & Manella, in Los Angeles, and my dad had just accepted a new post at the University of Southern California. Did you think I was going to stick around in Boston to find out what deeper levels of depravity Sam might be getting himself into as more time passed? I felt that he had gone down the Path of No Return, while I had landed on my feet. To each his own, as they say. It truly was good-bye forever.

EPILOGUE

JUNE 22, 1998

Upon getting on the plane headed for Los Angeles in June 1997, I felt like total shit. The plane ride was fine enough; all I had to do was sit there. But now, my funk would rebound into limitless vistas of euphoric cloudless bliss, as if the weight of the world had just been lifted from my shoulders, and I was free of whatever affliction had hindered me just moments previously. It was frightening; I didn't know who I was, the misery-prone Jay or the ebullient Jay, and there was no middle ground to choose from. For hours at a time, I would sit motionless and inert on the family room couch in my parents' new house in Los Angeles, unable to free myself from the strangling chokehold of what ailed me, until I would spot the family pet, and with a banshee-like scream, begin to give chase all over the house after our wily beagle June. I'm sure Mom and Dad suspected silently that something was amiss, while my brother Justin confided openly to them, "Wow, Harvard really screwed Jay up!" I became known in my family as the Brooding Philosopher.

This went on for nine very long months until I was fired from my job at the law firm for gross insubordination—trust me, you can only imagine the crazed antics I engaged in while flying high like a kite. Now I had no means to support myself. Their bewilderment turning into alarm, my parents planned for my 23rd birthday a lavish all-expenses paid vacation tour of the Grand Canyon, replete with dinghy rides on Lake Powell, views of the impressive Southern Rim, fine dining accommodations, sumptuous hotel stays, and the like. When even this didn't work, Dad, out of desperation, had me pay a visit to psychologist Dr. Edna, who had helped his colleague get over a messy divorce. Edna and I chatted quietly as I felt the pressure that had filled my skull slowly relieve itself. She scrawled the name and number of a Beverly Hills psychiatrist, Dr. Alan, for referral and consultation. I still remember that guy; he was constantly being interviewed on television shows on the major networks, he wielded a stellar professional reputation, and he was feared and admired by peers and colleagues alike. We sat down, he and I, and talked for half an hour, as I capitulated to his probing questions. Then he dropped a bomb on me.

"Jay, I spoke beforehand to Dr. Edna whom you saw a week ago," he began. "She made a definite diagnosis based on your visit with her, and I now concur with her diagnosis. You have Bipolar Disorder."

"Bipolar Disorder," I intoned robotically, mystified. "What is it?"

"It's a mood disorder, Jay. It used to be called Manic Depression. In your case, episodes of sadness alternate with episodes of irritability. Edna and I were very lucky to have identified it and corroborated each other's medical opinions so quickly."

"So how is it treated, Doctor? Can it be cured?"

"I'm sorry, Jay, there is no cure, although recovery is possible and the condition can go into remission," he told me. "It is best treated with a combination of therapy and medication. I'm going to start you out with Effexor and you should continue your visits with Edna," he said, handing me the script.

I stumbled out of the doctor's office, stunned by the prognosis as I made my way towards the parking lot. Boy, did I have a lot to think about. *How long will recovery take, if at all? Can I beat this challenge to my health and sanity? Do I have to take medication for the rest of my life? How do I make sense of this diagnosis?*

So, whereas before I had indulged my Passions, now I would have to govern them, and this time with the professional aid of physicians and clinicians along with pharmaceutical preparations and talk therapy, and not merely with the crude help of drugs and alcohol, or simply at the behest of parents and teachers.

In my silver coupe, a graduation present from Mom and Dad, and a valuable symbol of freedom in L.A., I sensed Fate in the passenger seat, smiling furtively. I had cheated her before many times, dared to challenge her, egged her on brazenly. But now she had played the ace up her sleeve: "No, Jay…the game's not over," she gloated and smirked. With Fate at my side, I cruised with the traffic, west on Wilshire Boulevard, windows down, through the heart of downtown Beverly Hills, feeling the windy heat of the first of many a Southern California summer, lowering the visor to shade my eyes from the blinding, blood-red rays of the setting West Coast sun…